Turo's Fated Mate

Iron Wolves MC
Book 7
By Elle Boon
elleboon@yahoo.com

© Copyright 2017 Elle Boon

All cover art and logos Valerie Tibbs of Tibbs Design ©
Copyright 2017 by Elle Boon
ISBN: 978-1-64136-817-9

Edited By Tracy Roelle
All rights reserved.

WARNING: The unauthorized reproduction or distribution of this copyrighted work is illegal. Criminal copyright infringement, including infringement without monetary gain, is investigated by the FBI and is punishable by up to 5 years in federal prison and a fine of $250,000.

Turo's Fated Mate, Iron Wolves MC Book 7
ISBN: 978-1-64136-817-9
Copyright © 2017 Elle Boon
First E-book Publication: August 2017
Cover design by Valerie Tibbs of Tibbs Design
Edited by Tracy Roelle

ALL RIGHTS RESERVED: This literary work may not be reproduced or transmitted in any form or by any means, including electronic or photographic reproduction, in whole or in part, without express written permission.

All characters and events in this book are fictitious. Any resemblance to actual persons living or dead is strictly coincidental.

Contents

Turo's Fated Mate 1

Dedication 5

Chapter One 7

Chapter Two 29

Chapter Three 52

Chapter Four 79

Chapter Five 95

Chapter Six 109

Chapter Seven 137

Chapter Eight 157

Chapter Nine 182

Chapter Ten 202

Chapter Eleven 227

Chapter Twelve 247

Chapter Thirteen 283

Chapter Fourteen 299

Chapter Fifteen 319

Chapter Sixteen 339

Chapter Seventeen 348

About Elle Boon 384

Other Books by Elle Boon 386

Dedication

I'd like to give a big, huge thank you to all my family and friends. Y'all have been such an amazing group who have kept me grounded through all the ups and downs. Without you, I'd have probably gone crazy this past year. Well, crazier anyhow.

Thank you to all who've read my stories and wanted more. I hope you enjoy Jenna the Fey Queen and her Wolpires aka the Cordell Twins book. I know that the road to a happily ever after isn't always smooth and hope I gave y'all one hell of a ride in their story. Stay tuned as the Dark Legacy Series is just beginning.

Of course, to my wonderful hubby who makes my life. Yep, I am saying he makes my life, because he does. Love you to the moon and back, Mr. Boon, 22 plus years and counting.

Love y'all so hard,
Elle

Chapter One

"Wow, wow, wow. Look at all these bikes." Jozlyn Rasey pulled her little pearl white Volkswagen Beetle between a huge pickup truck and a muscle car.

"Girl, I think your bug might stand out a bit." NeNe pushed open her door, straightening her shirt as she stood.

Joz rolled her eyes. "I'll have you know this is a 1971 VW Super Beetle. It's a classic." She ran her hand lovingly over the roof of her beloved car. She and her dad had rebuilt it when she'd told him she loved the old looking car one day when she'd been ten years old. It had taken them years to get it back to the pristine condition it was in today.

NeNe looked across the white top at her. "I think it's a great car. I'm just saying; around here, it definitely stands out a little."

She didn't care what anyone thought about her car or if it stood out amongst the motorcycles and big trucks. "Come on. Let's go meet little baby

Harlow and see about our friend, who somehow hid her pregnancy and relationship from us." There was no hiding the hurt and sense of betrayal she felt when she'd seen Lyric buying baby supplies then finding it was for her own child.

The sun going down brought a slight chill, a sense of foreboding. Joz looked around the empty parking lot, feeling as if someone or something was watching them.

"I wonder why she didn't want us to come to her house?" NeNe asked as she began walking toward the back of the club where Lyric worked.

Shrugging, Joz made sure the car was locked before following. In a pair of jeans and a tank top, she suddenly felt exposed. "Do you feel that?" she asked NeNe at the door marked Office.

"Feel what?" NeNe pulled the door open, waiting for Jozlyn.

"Never mind." She was being silly. The news of her grandmother's passing was affecting her, knowing she had to clear out the older woman's home and possibly find family shit she didn't want to find...well, anyone with a brain would be on edge.

"Hey, you two, come on in the back. Harlow is sleeping," Lyric Carmichael said.

Joz had to do a double take. Their friend was as fit as ever. "Alright, what gives?"

Lyric put her hands on her hips. "What do you mean?"

Waving her hand at Lyric, Joz sighed. "If you just had a baby then I'm Mother-Fucking Theresa."

"Watch your tone, girl."

Joz spun at the deep baritone coming from behind, her eyes widening at the sight of the huge man who'd entered without making a sound.

"Rowan Shade, be nice. These are the friends I told you about. Joz, NeNe, this is my m...fiancé Rowan. Rowan, these are my friends." Lyric held her hand out and damned if the huge man didn't go straight to Lyric, picking her up in a bear hug right in front of them.

It seemed like minutes would turn to hours before the man was ready to let Lyric go. Hell, if NeNe hadn't cleared her throat for the tenth time, or maybe the sleeping baby hadn't decided to let out a soft whimper, the man may have forgotten they were there all together.

"Aw, how's daddy's princess?" Rowan moved to where the now fussing baby lay.

Lyric mouthed *I'm sorry*, but her grin as she watched the big man, while he picked up his daughter, said she was happy. "She's ready to be fed, and unless you've grown some milk producing boobs, you're gonna need to hand her over."

"You know I like it when you get sassy, darlin," Rowan drawled, kissing the baby on her cheek as he handed her to Lyric.

The entire scene seemed unreal, like she was in an alternate reality. "What the fuckity fuck is going on here?" she blurted.

"Let me feed Harlow. And you," Lyric tilted her head at a growling Rowan before continuing. "You need to give me and my girls some privacy."

"Darlin, make no mistake, you get upset, I'll know it then there will be hell to pay. You and princess here are my world."

Watching as the big man brushed his lips over the baby's forehead, then Lyric's forehead, Joz glared as he stomped out the door.

"He's a little overprotective, but I promise he's really a sweetheart." Lyric gazed down at the baby who was trying to root for her milk. "Isn't that right? Yes, he is. Daddy thinks the sun rises and sets all because you're his princess."

Joz nodded. "That's what they said about..." NeNe put her hand over Joz's mouth.

"Don't get her started. Lord love this woman, but I swear university has done bad shit to her brain."

She shoved NeNe away, laughing at her accusation. Out of all their friends, she'd decided to go into psychology. The human mind was fascinating to her. However, now that she had graduated and been practicing for a couple years, the stress of patients was actually harder than she'd imagined. She'd never thought she was anything special, although she was younger by a couple years than the other girls, having an eidetic memory meant she moved up grades quickly, earning the nickname teacher's pet early on. Joz didn't mind being considered a geek, having a photographic memory came in handy. Heck, it actually helped keep her out of trouble, until she'd met Lyric and Syn. Now, those two were hell on wheels, and she loved them dearly. In her field, she chose child psychology as her professors had warned that adults wouldn't take to her being the one across from them. Whether it be a desk or chair, they'd see her as a kid.

"I can see that brain of yours working, trying to figure out how this happened," Lyric said as she sat down in an overstuffed chair adjusting her shirt then allowing her breast to peak out before the baby latched on.

"Well, there goes that theory." Joz bit her lip.

NeNe took a seat, looking around. "What were you thinking? 'Cause I can tell you I had a doozy worked up in my mind."

"You go first," Joz offered, sitting down next to NeNe. The sight of one tiny fist kneading the top of Lyric's breast and then Lyric quickly fitting her finger between the tiny fingers spoke of naturalness.

"Well, I was thinking she was playing a joke on us." NeNe shrugged and crossed one leg over the other.

Joz tilted her head to the side, meeting Lyric's brown eyes. "I thought maybe you'd taken in someone else's child and we were either gonna need to be your backup sitters, or your alibi. Now, since she's clearly yours, what with that mop of blonde hair and she looks like you and Hemsworth there, you gots some splaining to do, Lucy."

Lyric laughed, jarring the babe loose and causing her to cry out. She worked to shuffle Harlow to her other breast before responding. "Ok, so I'm totally loving the Hemsworth reference, but I'll keep that to myself. He doesn't need to get a big head, or bigger if ya know what I mean." Lyric winked.

"TMI, but please do go on." NeNe leaned forward.

"No, do not go on. Stop trying to distract with talk of your guy's package, big, small or otherwise." Joz had always known when Lyric was trying to blow her off and had allowed it since she'd preferred to stay in her bubble mostly. The few times she'd let loose, shit always got messed up. The last time she was out with the girls, Lyric had bugged out on them. "Wait, is that why you left us at the bar a few months back? Were you knocked up and didn't want us to know? You should've told us." Hell, it wasn't a big thing to be pregnant and not married in this day and age.

Lyric bit her lip. "I'm sorry. I should have told you sooner."

Joz got up and hugged Lyric and Harlow, who seemed to be done feeding. "Do you need to burp her, or can I?"

"You can, but she may not…" her words were interrupted by a healthy burp from Harlow as soon as Joz put the baby up to her shoulder.

"You were saying?" Joz asked, sitting down to look at the adorable little girl. "Wow, she's perfect. I mean, you must've been like six months along, but you weren't even showing, or you delivered early." Joz ran her finger down the soft cheek.

The sound of the door opening had them all looking up. A man as big as Lyric's fiancé walked in, but where Rowan was blond and dangerous in a boy next door way, this man was dark and menacing. He stood at well over six feet tall and had tattoos running down both arms. The dark sunglasses kept her from seeing what color his eyes were, but the black tank top with *Iron Wolves* on the front molded to his muscular chest, finishing off his bad boy looks was a pair of boots that beat against the hard wood with each step he took. She doubted anything escaped his notice, not even her indrawn breath as his head swiveled in her direction.

"Lyric, you got a number for the liquor supplier we use for the good stuff? We were short a couple cases."

His deep baritone sent a shiver down her spine. Joz tore her gaze away from the mountain of a man, focusing on the baby in her arms. Shit, if she didn't keep her mind out of the gutter, she'd start picturing him naked right in the middle of her friend's office. She most definitely didn't want to be caught drooling while holding a newborn.

"Name's Turo, what's yours?"

Joz gasped, wondering when he'd moved right in front of her. "Oh, I'm Jozlyn," she stammered. Jeezus tits on a boar. She never stammered.

"Jozlyn."

The way he said her name, sounded like a caress.

"Here you go, Turo." Lyric handed him a sheet of paper. "You should probably head back to the club and make that phone call." She nodded her head toward the door.

In all her twenty-two years, she'd never been drawn to any man who wasn't on television, but something tugged at her, telling her to follow where the stranger led. "Should I lay her down while she sleeps? I know some mothers think holding a baby all the time will spoil them, but in my professional opinion, that isn't true. In fact, there's new research from a psychologist friend of mine who studied more than five hundred people and found that those who were cuddled as children grew into more well-adjusted adults with less anxiety and had better mental health. They found that a positive childhood, along with cuddling, and lots of affection, combined with quality time also led to healthier adults with better coping skills." Jozlyn stopped as every eye in the room was staring at her as if she'd grown two heads. "What did I say?"

"You went all super smart soapbox woman on us," NeNe said, holding her arms out for the baby. "Let auntie NeNe hold the wee one since we clearly can't spoil by holding too much." She winked at Lyric.

"I'll have you know some of my work has been featured in journals, such as Applied Developmental Science, and I've added my own research on how the effects of cuddling helps preemies. Now others are seeing the benefits all the way up to adulthood. One day, I may be out of a job if everyone listens to me." Jozlyn glared at NeNe as she cooed down at Harlow.

"Clearly, I didn't get cuddled enough. When is my next session, Dr. Rasey?"

Jozlyn raised her middle finger on both hands.

"Did I tell you, Lyric, that brains turn me on?" Turo asked, his tone one of amusement.

"Turo, go." Lyric pointed toward the door.

When he turned away, Joz could've sworn his eyes had a blue hue to them, but when he turned back toward her, they were the obsidian black she'd first seen. How the hell did someone have such dark eyes?

Turo inhaled, the sweet smell of the tiny woman filling his senses with something akin to ambrosia. Fuck, his jeans got tight. Something he was sure wouldn't go unnoticed if the ladies glanced between his legs. Jozlyn. Her name, in and of itself, settled his wolf. Unlike Bodhi or Rowan, he was born a wolf, knowing full well his mate was somewhere out there. He just had to be patient. His patience had taken him all around the world, until something drew him to Kellen and his pack a little over fifteen years ago. Now, that something was within touching distance, only she was…breakable. How the hell could the Goddess give him a mate who was half his size and not a shifter?

"You're staring, big boy."

The sweet voice of the woman had his cock jerking. Fuck, he needed to get out of there before he did something he'd regret—like pick her up, throw her over his shoulder and take her back to his place. Nope, she was too sweet, too innocent, and way too young for the likes of him. Goddess be damned if he was taking a mate who he knew couldn't handle him. "I'm out. I'll take care of this." He nodded at the paper then beat feet to the door. Once outside he took in a lungful of air, hoping to rid himself of the sweet scent of his mate, cause fuck it all, that's who she was.

Striding to the back door of the club, he wasn't surprised to find Coti at the door. The other man seemed to have a sixth sense when it came to him.

"Yo, Turo, what's wrong man?" Coti asked, his dark eyes bore into Turo's.

He tilted his head back and forth then side to side, the snap, crackle, and pop sound overly loud. "Nothing. I need you to do me a solid and handle the bar for a couple days. Oh, and we were short a couple cases of Jameson. Here's the number for the distributor. Give them a call and tell them they got twenty-four hours to make it right or we're changing who we get our liquor from." Fuck it all, if they didn't send the correct amount, he was liable to go there and get the shortened number himself. Yeah, he needed to take a break far away from the Iron Wolves and his…he wasn't even going there.

Jozlyn Rasey wasn't his. He wouldn't even say it inside his head. Mind over matter, his mind was like a steel trap, once he set it on something it was done. After hundreds of years on earth, Turo knew he could forget about the tiny dynamite of a woman. He just needed a little space. Like a few hundred miles, maybe thousands.

"Sure, and pigs might fly, too," he muttered.

"What's got you by the short hairs?" Coti looked at the door that Turo had exited, it's thickness blocked him from seeing what was on the other side.

Turo regretted being short with his friend. "Sorry, I just need to clear my head. I'll only be gone a few days, a week at the most. If you need me, I'll have my cell, but only if it's an emergency."

Coti raised a dark brow. "You tell Kellen yet?"

He scrubbed his hand over his jaw. "Not yet. No worries, he'll understand." Turo hoped his alpha did, otherwise he'd move on permanently. Fuck, he might be doing that anyhow, what with the little minx and Lyric being tight and all. He had great will power but being forced into close proximity and unable to take what he knew was his, was pushing his limit.

Coti narrowed his eyes. "Bullfuck, man. I can see determination in your eyes, and it ain't saying the same shit coming out of your mouth. Pledge you'll come back, even if it's to say goodbye."

The stubborn set to his best friend's jaw said he'd either not give in, or he'd be following Turo wherever he went. Not that he didn't think he could lose Coti in a matter of hours, but he didn't want to hurt their friendship, or the other wolf's pride. "I swear I'll be back."

"I suppose that's as good as I'll be getting." A tick worked in Coti's jaw. Anger and something akin to sadness clouded his features.

Turo nodded and clapped him on the shoulder. "A hui kaua." The traditional Hawaiian saying of 'until we meet again' rolled off his tongue."

"A hui hou," Coti said, saying almost the same thing, adding a goodbye to the 'until we meet again', clearly telling Turo he wasn't letting him off the hook. He opened the door to the bar, holding it open as he stared at Turo.

With one last look at the dark interior of the bar, he made eye contact with a few of the shifters, tilting his head in greeting then turned to leave without another word.

His custom Harley Nighttrain, which was all blacked out with a mustang cobra solo seat and 3" extended controls, beckoned him. He'd changed the drag bars and risers to accommodate his larger frame, and now, he could comfortably ride for hundreds of miles, which would suit him just fine for the coming days.

At the back of the lot, the sound of feminine voices floated to him, but one voice resonated loudest. With a growl, he flung his leg over the seat and started his bike. The deep rumble matched the one vibrating in his chest. His primal beast inside clawed at him, needing its mate. Turo forced it back into submission. He was the master not the other way around.

Not bothering to put his skullcap on, he used his legs to back out of the spot he was in, turning after he was in the clear. With a few revs of the engine, he roared out of the lot. Once he was home and had a small bag packed, he'd contact Kellen. If worse comes to worst and his alpha said he couldn't go, he'd sever ties to the Iron Wolves. The more he thought about it, the more he thought the idea had merit. Hell, it was probably time he did just that. An image of Jozlyn popped into his mind, making him nearly crash. Only his quick reflexes and superior skill kept him from laying the bike on the hard asphalt that made up the highway.

Pressing a button on the console, Motionless In White's *Loud* began blaring through the speakers. His mind cleared as the words of the song resonated inside him. The chorus 'Fuck it' had him nodding his head. Yeah, he was totally on board with being crass and turning shit up.

Twenty minutes later and several songs more, the driveway to his place came into view. Like the other members of his pack, he preferred a place with privacy. Unlike many of his pack, he didn't stay as close to the alpha or the rest of them, mainly because he was older and didn't want to deal with the inevitable questions they might ask. He opened his senses as the bike ate up the final yards to his front porch, checking for any signs someone had been near his home. His wolf growled, unhappy he'd not gotten to rub up against their mate. Turo wasn't happy either, but it was best for all of them. Hell, the tiny Japanese looking woman had no clue just what she'd stepped into. He wondered how she'd become friends with Lyric and Syn. It didn't matter. He wouldn't allow it to matter. The more he thought about it, the more he came to the conclusion he wouldn't be coming back to South Dakota. At least not while Jozlyn was around. Maybe in sixty or seventy years. After she was old enough to have moved on, made a family of her own. A deep, angry growl bubbled out of him. The image of another man claiming what was his had his claws extending, fur popping out along his arms.

Fuck it all, he needed to get his shit and get gone. Distance was what he needed. Even miles away he could smell her sweet ambrosia, like the sweetest mango on the islands of Hawaii.

The song by Breaking Benjamin, *Never Again,* was on as he parked next to his house. The words 'I beat for you. You bring me back to life' seemed to have a meaning all of its own. An owl flew overhead, landing on a branch. Turo glared at the bird whose eyes mocked him in return.

He lifted his finger and flipped the owl off before going inside to pack. The sooner he hit the road, the quicker he'd leave thoughts of one dark eyed, silky black-haired female behind. His dick jerked behind the fly of his jeans. He ignored the ache, tossing a couple pairs of jeans and T-shirts into a bag along with bathroom necessities. Not that he needed more than a toothbrush and toothpaste along with shampoo. He'd pick up anything else he needed once he got to where he was going.

Opening his mind to the link with Kellen, he waited for his chosen alpha to answer. With the man's wife due any time, he was pretty positive he wouldn't be interrupting their sexy time but was still cautious not to intrude.

"What's doin', Turo?"

"I'm heading out for a bit. Need to clear my head," he answered.

Silence met his words for several long seconds. *"You coming back?"*

Turo pinched the bridge of his nose, exhaling when he felt he could answer without sounding like a complete liar. *"Not sure just yet."*

"You're always part of my pack, regardless of miles or years, Turo. You go get your head on straight. Come back when you feel it's time. Remember something though…time doesn't always wait on us."

He wanted to laugh but knew it wouldn't be appropriate. *"Thanks for the advice. Take care of you and yours. Give Lake and the team, when they come, a kiss from me."*

"That sounds pretty permanent," Kellen growled.

"I'm not sure yet. I'll let you know." Turo picked up his bag, looking around the sparse interior. After fifteen years, he hadn't changed much except replacing the furniture a couple times and buying new kitchen things when needed. *"You'll be the first to know what I decide."* It was the only promise he could give Kellen at the time.

A deep rumble was his answer. Turo severed the link before he said anything that would constitute as an affront to the alpha, not that Kellen really gave two fucks, but he still wouldn't show disrespect, much. Hell, he was hundreds of years older than the Iron Wolf, but he gave a pledge and would honor it. For the time being.

Chapter Two

Jozlyn stared at the closed door, her heart hammering against her ribs. "Holy shit, who was that man?"

Lyric put her hand on her arm, startling her. "That was Turo, and way too much man for you, young lady."

Hearing her friend say what everyone always said, hurt. She'd been told since grade school she wasn't normal. Always being the smart girl. One of the smallest in the group kept her from forming friendships, until high school when Lyric and Syn had taken her under their wings. Now it seemed they didn't think she was good enough for their friend, or at least Lyric didn't. She tried not to let the older girl see how her words hurt. "I'm not in the market for a man so don't worry I'd taint your friend with my weirdness, Lyric. Oh, would you look at the time. I need to get going, I've got a patient appointment in an hour. NeNe, you coming with or staying?" NeNe wasn't weird like her.

They'd probably let her stay and get to know any man she wanted.

"Joz, it's not what you think," Lyric began.

She fumbled for the keys in her bag, pasting a smile on her face. "Of course not. I was just kidding. Your baby is adorbs for real. I'll come back when I have more time," she promised. Or when hell froze over. Yeah, the former was more like it. She didn't realize her *friends* didn't think she was good enough for their men friends. The hurt went deep. Not that she thought a man like Turo would actually want her, but one could always fantasize dammit.

Moving quickly toward the door, she ignored Lyric's protests, her eyes watering with unshed tears. NeNe held little Harlow, which meant she didn't have to wait for her either. At a quick pace, she slammed out of the office, paying no attention to Lyric as she called for her.

"I'll see you, Lyric," she yelled. The sound of a growl reached her ears, making the fine hairs on her arms stand on end. A man who resembled Turo opened the door to the bar, only this one had his head shaved. She shivered at the intense look aimed her way. His dark gaze went back toward Lyric who stood in the doorway with Harlow in her arms, the baby crying. NeNe staring at him with a look of awe. Yeah, go ahead and eat him up, she thought. NeNe wasn't a freak like Jozlyn was.

Her little VW rumbled to life. Without stirring up any gravel, she eased out of the lot, waving as if she hadn't just lost a couple friends. Who the heck was she kidding. She'd just lost her only friends, save for maybe NeNe, who probably thought she was acting juvenile for running off like she'd done.

Taking a deep breath, she swiped her fingers under her right eye then her left, erasing the tears. "Chin up, girl. Big girls don't cry." Looking in the rearview mirror for the last time, she didn't breathe easily until the club was no longer visible. She changed lanes on the highway, ignoring the ache in her chest. Her mind filed the last hour into a box in a corner of her brain. That was how she dealt with things. Each and everything she did had a purpose and a place. Organization and focus. She pulled up the file of her next patient. Nancy Lee. An eleven-year-old child from a single home being raised by her father. Her mother died when she was six. A fall down the family's steps, breaking her neck. The little girl was the one to find her, leaving mental scars that plagued the young child. She wasn't the first case Jozlyn had dealt with where the patient had emotional trauma, but something about the case had her protective instinct on alert. Nancy had tried to commit suicide three times, the last time she'd almost succeeded. Jozlyn didn't plan to let there be a fourth. Thinking about work kept her from dwelling on her own problems as she pulled into her designated spot at the hospital where Nancy was being held for a thirty-day evaluation. That gave them both time to get to know one another. Hopefully, it also gave them time to build trust.

She pulled her badge out of the glove compartment, grabbed her purse, and got out of her car. Inserting her key, she locked the driver's door. The feel of being spied on made her turn around in the almost empty lot. Seeing nothing, she hurried to the door where she swiped her card to gain entrance. The guard on duty nodded at her as she passed. "Evening Greg. How's it going?"

"Not too bad, Dr. Rasey, thank you for asking. It's quiet tonight, which is a good thing around here." Gregg stood with his arms crossed near the elevators where he could see the front doors and the hallway leading to the entrance to the patient floors.

"Great news. I'll be in my office, if anyone needs me." A sense of calmness stole over her as she pushed the button to the fourth floor. Not many other people were working, since it was a Saturday, but she wasn't considered normal. Heck, she'd never been normal if you ask anyone in her family. As if she'd conjured her dad up, her phone rang, the caller ID showing it was her dad's cell phone. "Hello," she answered on the third ring.

"How's my baby girl?" Patrick Rasey's deep baritone asked.

She sat down in her ergonomic office chair, looking at the calendar she kept on her desk even though she also kept one on her phone. She'd need to hurry if she was going to make it up to visit with her patients before her next appointment. "I'm good, dad. How's mom?"

"She's off running errands. You know how she likes to go to the market when I'm not home," he sighed.

Her mother loved going to the farmer's market and getting fresh vegetables instead of ones at the store. "Yes, and you love eating what she creates with the goodies she buys. Listen, I need to make a few visits before my next session. I'll call you when I get home tonight."

"Joz, you haven't come over for a proper dinner in weeks. Your mother and I miss you." Patrick Rasey knew how to lay on the guilt.

A gentle laugh escaped. "Daddy, I was just there three days ago. I'll call when I get home and see what's for dinner tomorrow night. Are you going to be home?" If she knew her dad, which she totally did, he'd make sure her mother prepared her favorite gyoza from scratch along with a few other traditional Japanese treats. However, the fried dumplings were her favorite.

"Yes, unless something happens. Give your mother a call. I'll talk to you then. Don't forget," Patrick admonished.

His words made her laugh. Having an eidetic memory, Jozlyn didn't forget anything. She replaced the handset before getting up and tucking her purse into the bottom drawer of her desk. Her cell fit into the pocket of her white doctor's jacket, the one she felt made her appear older and wiser.

With her badge clipped to the lapel, she headed toward the bank of elevators at the other end of the hall, leading to the psych ward. Once inside, she had to swipe her badge to gain access, since they kept the floors locked down in order to ensure the patients safety as well as keeping them from escaping. The entire process seemed a little overkill to her, but she understood the need in some cases. However, the ones she dealt with usually were misunderstood or had suffered some kind of trauma. Flipping through her mental files, she pulled up the cases she would be seeing. Nancy Lee followed by Aleria, a young woman who was being held until they could safely say she was sane to stand trial for murder. From what Joz had seen, Aleria was most definitely sane. She was just pushed past a young girl's limits and killed an abusive parent. However, the courts didn't agree, hence the defense team had her plead insanity. The next file she pulled up in her mind was of a drug addicted young man. He was a few years younger than she was, but whatever he'd been using ate away at him, making him hate everyone, including himself to the extent he tried to kill himself. Now, he was under observation after finishing detox.

   The last case she was going to see was a young girl named Egypt. She also tried to commit suicide, but luckily for her, a neighbor had seen through the bathroom window and had called 911. The twelve-year-old would always carry the scars on her wrists from where she'd taken a kitchen knife to them, yet she was alive. If Joz had her way, she'd find a way to convince the girl to talk to her. She'd read the reports and was intrigued when the other case workers had said they couldn't get the girl to answer a single question, not even what her name was. Well, she wasn't like the others.

"Hi, Pam. Quiet around here. Is it a full moon or what?" Joz looked around the nurses' area that usually had three or four nurses, noticing Pam was alone.

Pam shrugged. "It's Colleen's birthday. Everyone's in the breakroom having cake, so I volunteered to watch the front. You should poke your head in and see if there's any left. Amy made her special Devil's Food cake with strawberries and cool whip on top."

"That sounds delicious. When I'm finished with my patients, I'll check it out." She hated the term 'patient', always wanted to call them her people instead. She'd been told it made them feel more like human beings by a former patient, but the hospital frowned on the familiarity.

"Alright, but if it's all gone, don't say I didn't warn you. Oh, by the way, one of your patients,

Nancy Lee was taken back down to Intensive Care due to an infection."

Joz looked at her watch, then grimaced. "Oh, thanks for letting me know. Talk to you in a bit." She left the nurses area, heading toward Aleria's room. She gave a brief knock and waited before she entered. Even though they were essentially prisoners, she still gave them the respect she'd want.

Aleria eyed her as she walked in. "Who the hell are you, Punky Brewster?"

A snort escaped Joz. "I'd almost be offended, except I've seen reruns of that old show. I'm Dr. Rasey. How're you today? May I call you Aleria?"

"I don't think I'm in any position to stop you. Are you truly a doctor, or am I being punked? Being crazy doesn't give anyone the right to punk you," she whispered.

Joz took in the fact Aleria's arms were fastened to the bars of the bed. "Why are you strapped to the bed like that?"

Aleria gave a cackling laugh. "Why, because I'm a nut, and I kill people. Didn't you read your notes, Dr Doogette Howser."

"You seem to be able to remember shows from the 80's. Are you a fan of that time?" Joz kept her tone neutral.

"I also love the music from the 80's. Want me to start singing you a little GNR?" Aleria jerked her arms, cursing when they didn't release from the straps. "I fucking hate these things. I hate all of you people."

For the next half hour she listened to Aleria talk, listened as she yelled, and then the young girl calmed as she realized Joz wasn't rising to any of her baiting.

"What is wrong with you? Why are you still here, and why haven't you taken a fucking note?" The last was asked in a loud growl.

Joz shrugged. "I'm here because that's my job, and I love my job. I don't need to take notes, because I have a great memory."

Aleria fell back against the pillows. "Oh really. What kind allows you to remember everything I just told you?"

"It's like a photographic memory. I have the ability to recall just about anything I see, hear, or am exposed to. Some who have eidetic don't have true photographic memory, but I do, so I guess I'm a freak of nature. Eidetic memory is referred to as those being able to view memories like a photograph, whereas those with a photographic memory can recall pages of text or numbers and such. I can do both." Joz watched to see how Aleria would react to her words.

"Holyfuckingshit, how do you function if you are always assimilating knowledge?"

The fact Aleria came up with a question that wasn't elementary showed she wasn't insane. However, she could've been temporarily insane. There are many cases, but what this woman should be pleading is irresistible impulse. Shit, she wasn't her lawyer, yet wanted to help Aleria.

"The same as you. My mind just works differently. To me, what I do is no different than breathing for you." Her phone vibrated in her pocket, the silent message that time was up.

"Sure, and donkeys fly out my ass," Aleria agreed.

Joz stood and walked over to the window. The parking lot looked the same as when she'd come in. "Aleria, you realize you could've had a mental break from the trauma you'd suffered, yes? I mean your lawyer has probably looked into every aspect of your case, I'm sure." Joz mentioned the impulse factor, watching Aleria's eyes widen.

"I...I'm not sure. I'll ask my aunt and him at our next visit."

"Ask them what? I mean I didn't say anything you surely hadn't already thought of. You're a smart girl who's been knocked down. You just need to dust your hands off before you move forward." Sure, she'd killed her drug addicted mother who'd tried to whore her daughter out, but Joz couldn't miss the swelling that was still apparent in the girl's face, nor had she missed the hospital records from the numerous falls Aleria had taken or the rape kit results. How nobody had seen there was something wrong when a child had broken both arms and several ribs, plus her nose three times, enough that she'd actually needed plastic surgery to repair the damage done to her face but claimed she was clumsy, was beyond Joz. And all those breaks had occurred since the girl's mother had divorced her husband. Yeah, she was sure Aleria was temporarily insane when she'd shoved the woman down the stairs. She patted Aleria's hand with a promise she'd see her soon, walking out with hope that Aleria would talk with her lawyer and aunt with the words Jozlyn had given her.

Next up was Mick. She sighed, knowing even before she went into his room he was going to be a lost cause. Some sixth sense told her things like that, but she still entered the room with her usual smile.

"If you've come to tell me how much I'm wasting my life, you can turn around and go get fucked. I'm aware what kind of suckhole on humanity I am. Trust me, I've heard it all before." The thin young man with the buzzcut glared at her.

"Suckhole on humanity, huh? That's a first for me. How's your head feeling today?" Joz indicated the large bandage on his forehead.

He touched his head. "It's been better. Aren't you going to tell me not to be...I don't know, such a downer?"

"Seems like a waste of time. I figure I'd just sit here and watch you for the next," she looked at her phone, checking the time. "Half hour or so."

Mick laughed. "You've got balls; I'll give you that."

"I've been told that before."

The next half hour passed quickly, and then it was time to meet with her last patient. Egypt Light. She took a deep breath before entering the little girl's room. After her customary knock and wait, she walked in. Egypt lay on the bed. Her caramel skin and liquid brown eyes made her think of Turo.

She pushed thoughts of the big man aside and studied the wan face looking back at her.

Stubbornness radiated from the too thin face. Yeah, she could totally see how this little sprite was able to hold her tongue when spoken to. "Hiya, Egypt. My name is Dr. Rasey. How are you today?"

Nothing. Not anything to indicate the girl cared.

She walked around the foot of the bed and looked out the window. From this view Joz could see the front of the hospital. The parking lot was now filled to bursting, but being on the upper floors, they appeared like toy cars instead of real ones below. "I think there's a firetruck down below. That usually means one of their friends were hurt," Joz mentioned without turning around.

"Do you like My Little Ponies, or are you into big girl things like makeup and stuff? When I was your age I liked unicorns. I still do, actually. My mom kept all my books I collected when I was a kid. We're talking stacks of them where I loaded them up with stickers of unicorns and rainbows. She said someday I could give them to my daughter.

What do you think? Would you want old books like that from your mom?"

A swift inhale proceeded the girl's head turning away, but Joz noticed tears in the dark eyes. "I told her she could keep them at her place and give them to charity, or whatever. I couldn't see a kid of mine wanting them. Of course, I don't have any kids, nor do I see any in the near future."

"That was rude of you. If your mom was nice enough…" Egypt trailed off.

"Yeah, I guess you're right. I should apologize. My mom only wanted to savor those memories, and who knows, one day, so will I with my own daughter. Thank you for helping me see I was being a brat." Joz kept her back to Egypt but could see her image through the window.

"I'm not a brat. I'm a good girl. I try so hard, but daddy…" her words trailed off as she bit her lip.

"Anything you say to me is confidential, Egypt. I have sworn an oath."

Egypt looked down at her wrists, glaring at the bandages covering them. "Why won't the pain stop?"

Joz's heart broke for the young girl. "Pain comes in all shapes and sizes. It's how we deal with it that's the true test of our strength."

"I'm tired of pain. Tired of…everything. Why did my momma leave me here alone?" Egypt curled on her side, crying ragged tears that ripped at her heart.

Joz wanted to find the girl's mother and beat the shit right out of her. "I don't know, nugget. I don't know."

By the time she left Egypt's room, she felt physically and emotionally worn. Egypt promised to talk to her every day and even agreed to counselling outside of the hospital. Joz wasn't sure what their finances were like, but she'd make for damn sure the courts mandated Egypt was to see her twice a week. It was good to have a dad who not only loved you, but also happened to be a retired judge. If only he didn't travel so much doing god knew what, but that was her dad.

"I saved you a piece of cake," Pam said.

Joz looked at the large slice of yummy goodness and accepted the treat with a smile. "I'm gonna take it to my office to enjoy. Thanks for saving it for me. Did you get one?"

Pam nodded. "Heck yeah. You think you'd be getting one if I didn't?" Pam's laugh was genuine.

"Well, alright then. I see where I stand."

"Yep, behind cake. Always, behind cake."

"You working tomorrow?" Joz asked as she walked backward, her plate of cake held against her stomach.

"Nope. I'm off for the next week. Vacation, baby." Eyes twinkling, Pam opened her mouth to say something but stopped as the phone rang. "Gotta get that. Talk to you soon."

Taking the elevator back to her office, she settled behind her computer, making notes in each of the three charts online. She really wanted to find out more about Egypt's life. One thing was certain…her home wasn't a bed of roses or at least not ones without thorns. Once she was finished making notes, she sat back with a sigh, thinking about her friends Lyric and Syn. In the last few months she'd felt a chasm had come between them. NeNe had said the same thing. Clearly Lyric had been keeping a huge secret, but a baby was more than what she'd expected. Heck, they'd gone out to a local bar less than six months ago.

She closed her eyes, thinking back to the night they'd all gone out. Of course, she'd allowed NeNe to talk her into wearing a short skirt and a tiny top, showing off more skin than she'd covered. Not that she hadn't gotten a lot of attention, more than she'd ever gotten before when they'd gone out. Lyric had disappeared shortly after they'd gotten there. Joz was sure they'd all drank a shot or two, even Lyric. Her mind was like a steel trap, having her memory was a blessing and a curse. So, either Lyric didn't know she was preggo, or she was really irresponsible. Joz couldn't think her friend would be that type of person, which meant she hadn't known then.

"Damn what's it matter? Water under the bridge and all that."

Her phone rang, startling her from her thoughts. Seeing her mother's number made her smile. "Hi, mom. What's up?"

"Can't a mother call her only child without something being up?" Noriko Rasey harrumphed.

"Mother, you and I both know you. Spill," Jozlyn said.

"Fine, I had a feeling you needed to talk to someone. Feel better?"

An image of her mother crossing her arms over her chest while she glared at the wall had Jozlyn smiling. "I love you mama." The reality that not everyone was blessed with parents like hers always amazed her.

"Love you too, Utsukushī musume. Now, tell me what's wrong," Noriko ordered.

Her mother always called her beautiful daughter in Japanese. The sense of normalcy had her closing her eyes as a wealth of love flowed over her. "I have several new cases, which I can't tell you about, but one of them broke my heart today."

"I always said you were much too kind hearted for that type of job. Why you didn't just find a nice young man and settle down was always baffling to me. But…before you go into your usual explanations about how you wanted to make a difference, why don't you pack up for the night and come have dinner with me? Your dad is out of town at a conference of some sort." Her mother harrumphed again.

Laughing, she agreed. Her mother didn't try to keep track of where her father went since he travelled a lot, but they always spoke at least twice a day no matter where her dad was. "I'll see you in an hour. Do you need me to pick anything up?"

"Nope, unless you want to sleep over then I have everything else." Longing tinged her mother's voice.

"I have to do rounds at the hospital tomorrow, or I'd love to stay with you. Maybe next time," she promised.

"See you soon. Drive safe and buckle up. I'm sure you will, but I have to say it anyways."

Jozlyn laughed cause her mother always said the same thing, and yes, she always buckled up and obeyed the speed limits. She couldn't wait to see her mom, eat a home cooked meal, and file today away in a folder in her mind. Some days she wished she didn't have the memory she did. Today was one of those days, as she pictured Egypt's tear streaked face. "Stop it. Focus on food and your mom," she admonished herself as she grabbed her purse out of the bottom drawer after she logged off her computer. Tomorrow, she'd start fresh and be ready to face a new batch of patients.

Chapter Three

Turo eased off the throttle, letting the bike roll to a stop. He'd been riding for several hours, could ride for a few more, but something was calling him, that same thing that had led him to the Iron Wolves, a sense that he'd always heeded.

The park he passed had a parking lot that was surprisingly full of vehicles, mostly out of town plates; he noted. He continued until he came to a clearing with just enough room, that he could maneuver his bike.

Now, he allowed his wolf to surface a little, letting his heightened senses work as he sniffed, trying to filter out the smells of fuel and grease from vehicles. Men and their attempt at grilling smelled as if they were competing with the highway, trying to make smoke signals or some shit, making it hard for most to smell anything except the scent of barbeque.

The acrid scent of fear hit him, making his wolf and him both stand on his idling Harley. Pressing the stand down, he swung off his bike, lifting his nose until he could pinpoint where the smell was coming from. Years before he found the Iron Wolves, he travelled from one place to the next, looking for something, always finding trouble, or trouble found him. The last thing he wanted to do was bust into a cabin or tent and beat the shit out of someone. His boots barely made a sound as he ghosted over dried leaves, his muscles tensing the closer he got to the door where the smell was the strongest. His fists were curled, ready to beat the fuck out of whoever caused the emotions leaking out to him from the female. Turo was silent as he stepped onto the rickety porch, noting the deplorable condition of the place. A squirrel looked up with an acorn in its paws, skittering away as it realized it was no longer alone.

Standing outside he heard a muffled sob. His senses picked up only one heartbeat inside. The woman's fear ate at him, but he wasn't sure if he should knock, call the cops, or leave her be. If he knocked, she could be unable to answer. If he called the cops, they might think he was a stalker or some shit. Hell, he was well over six feet tall, with more tattoos than most, and drove a Harley. Not to mention, he had a cut on proclaiming him part of an MC. Yeah, option two was out. Leaving wasn't an option for him either. The Goddess led him there, just as he knew she'd taken him to the Iron Wolves.

He knocked then waited. When silence greeted him, he sighed. "My name is Arturo. I know you're in there, and you're scared. I'm here to help you." Shit, he couldn't help how deep and growly his voice was. He hoped like hell the woman didn't freak the fuck out and start screaming the place down or call the cops herself. He'd hate like all get out to have to explain why he was there. When seconds stretched into a good two minutes, he knocked again. "Listen, I know you're in there. I want to help, but I can't if you don't let me."

He'd give her another thirty seconds, then he'd do a little B&E. Wouldn't be the first, nor the last he was sure.

"Just a heads up, if you don't open the door, I'm gonna have to break in, which I really don't want to do. I'll then have to reimburse whoever owns this...place for any damage I do to their door. I'm tired, dirty, and a little stressed. However, I give you my word I will not hurt you." He couldn't make it any clearer, but he was done standing outside talking through the door. He was shocked when it turned without resistance. The sight that met his eyes was not what he'd expected. The thin, bruised, bloody woman on the bed looked to be near death. "Fuckmerunnin'," he muttered.

Large brown eyes blinked, yet no tears formed. He wasn't sure if it was due to the lack of moisture in her clearly emancipated form, or that she'd finally given up. "Sweetheart, I'm gonna kill the fucker who did this to you," he promised.

Fear and hope brightened her eyes, but the filthy rag over her mouth kept her from saying anything.

"I'm afraid to touch you, but I have to get this out of the way." As gently as he could, he tried to untie the gag from her mouth. The bastard had knotted it into her hair, effectively keeping it in place. "I need to cut this off you. You cool with that?"

The young woman lay back, her muscles tensing as he pulled a blade from his back pocket. Turo opened the wicked looking knife, showing her what he was doing. Knowing nothing he could do would completely alleviate her fears, he inserted the knife between her cheek and the cloth, slicing it cleanly away. Her mouth was so dry he feared he'd tear bits of her lips if he tried to move the gag away. "Let me get some water to wet the cloth before we try to remove it." He went to the bathroom and wet a washrag, noticing the filthy state it had been left in.

In moments, he was back with the cloth and had moistened the gag. Goddess, he wasn't sure what the fuck he was going to say or what she'd say. Only knew he needed to be prepared for the worst. The bastard or bastards had beaten her within an inch of her life and left her tied down to the bed with ropes wrapped around her from collar bone to ankles. She didn't appear to be able to move, but the coarse ropes were biting into her naked bleeding flesh. Hell, she'd scar for sure, but that would be the least of her injuries.

"My baby," she whispered once they'd worked the cloth out of her mouth.

Turo looked around the room, not seeing a child or smelling one. "What's your name? What's your kid's name?" he asked.

"Asia and Egypt," she replied.

The unusual names had him squinting down at the dark-skinned beauty. Even beat to hell and back, he could tell she had been beautiful before the ordeal. "Do you have a husband or family I should call?"

Fear, the scent like acid, washed over him. Her head jerked back and forth. "No, please help me." Her injuries had to be life threatening, yet she thrashed about.

"Stop it, you're hurting yourself." Turo tried to sound kind. But fuck him, his wolf wanted to rip into whoever had done this to the woman.

With trembling lips, she stilled. "Help me, please," she rasped, passing out before he could reassure her.

Turo glared at the room, opening his senses. He could smell a human male along with the woman's scent. The man's smell had been gone for days at least. How could he have beaten this woman and left her in such a state? Knowing time wasn't on his side. For one thing, he didn't know the woman. For two, he didn't know when the man who'd done this to her would be returning. For three, if the man did return, he knew he'd probably kill him with his bare hands, which would probably land him on the wrong side of the human law. And last but certainly not least, he didn't know who the hell she was or who did this to her. Turo sighed as he looked down at the woman. He needed his alpha, and he needed the help of the Fey Queen for sure. Then, he was going hunting. This woman was an unknown to him, but he'd been drawn to the location a few hours outside of the packs territory. Whatever it was, he'd figure it out then he'd get back on his bike.

Opening his mind, he tapped into the link to his alpha for the second time in the last twenty-four hours. Hell, the way things were going, Kellen was going to tell him to get fucked.

"This is clearly not a social call. What's up?"

With as few words as possible, he explained the situation to Kellen then waited.

"Well, shit, son, you sure know how to go riding into trouble. Let me get in touch with Jenna. If anyone can pop in and out, it's her. Should you warn your friend first?"

"Nah, she's out. I'm worried 'cause it seems she's been alone and tied down for at least a couple days without food or water. She's in pretty bad shape." He allowed Kellen to see through his eyes, letting the alpha see what condition the woman on the bed was in. Luckily, she wasn't naked, but her clothes were bloody and soiled.

"Fucking shit, she looks like she's been beaten by a sledge hammer. Has she spoken?" Kellen's

growled question had Turo moving to listen for her breathing pattern.

He exhaled loudly. *"Yeah. I'm not sure if she's Asia or Egypt, but I got the clear impression those are names, not places she was saying."*

"Jenna should be coming shortly. I'd come too, but Laikyn has been having more labor pains. I'm not sure if I'm gonna make it through this pregnancy," Kellen swore.

"Thousands of men every hour of every day say the same thing. You're just freaked cause you're not able to take her pain into you nor control what's happening," Turo said with the knowledge he knew exactly what his alpha was going through. Although he'd not been in Kellen's shoes, he'd been around long enough to have witnessed enough fathers-to-be freaking out. Although, most didn't have their mates go from a couple months to almost nine in the blink of an eye, thanks to a little visit to the Fey realm like Kellen's mate Laikyn. And most didn't have their mate pregnant with more than one yet unable to find out exactly how many thanks to the

children in her stomach having some major magic already. Yeah, Kellen definitely wasn't normal nor were his children.

"I see you're rethinking your thoughts," Kellen muttered.

"Hey, you're a lucky bastard to have found your mate so soon. Not everyone can say the same." Turo immediately realized he'd said too much. The silence on the other end of the link stretched.

"You realize you can tell me anything. I've never pried. I respect you and your privacy as your friend and alpha, but I know there's more to you than just the man I met fifteen years ago," Kellen replied.

Turo took a deep breath. *"I need to go. She's stirring. I'll update you on her condition."*

Kellen's grunt was exactly what he'd expected as he cut their connection.

A small light burst in the room before Jenna, the Fey Queen, appeared. Her usual bubbly persona disappeared the moment she locked eyes on the prone form in the bed. "Goddess," she whispered.

"That's a lot milder than what I said," Turo agreed.

Jenna gazed at him, pinning him with an intense stare. "Whoever did this to her needs to pay."

"At least we're on the same page." He nodded toward the woman. "Can you fix her?"

"Pfft, but of course. However, I don't want to do it here, nor do I think we should just take her without her consent." Jenna bit her lip. "Shoot, what a conundrum. Well, nothing to do but do it. I'll just take her with me in a bubble so my time doesn't mess with her time, get her fixed up right as rain," Jenna muttered, her hands moving over the entire bed.

"Yo, Jenna, wanna explain what you're doing to those who are new to the class?" Turo stood with his hands on his hips, wondering what the heck the crazy Fey was doing.

The Fey Queen narrowed her eyes at him. A lesser man would have cowered at the intense look, but he'd been around the block a few hundred years and didn't scare as easily as a young pup.

"Oh, you're not what you appear, are you?" Jenna dusted her hands together, tilting her head to the side. "No, you're older, not like in an old soul but an older wolf," she paused as she tapped her index finger on her lip. "You're a riddle to me, but I'll figure you out. Give me time or just spill and save us both the energy."

His lips kicked up in an involuntary grin. Jennaveve was truly too cute for words. Of course, he knew she could squash him like a bug. He'd seen her literally roll an entire compound without breaking a sweat, yet she treated them all as if they were equals...sort of. When she finally accepted her mates, he couldn't wait to see the hell she'd give them.

The woman on the bed moaned, drawing both their attentions and saving him from the inquisition.

"You're not off the hook my big fish," Jenna warned.

Yeah, she was scary even though she barely reached his chest.

Jozlyn woke refreshed. A night of relaxing with her mother always made all her stress and worries fade away. After glancing at her clock, she sprang out of bed thirty minutes before her alarm was set to go off, quickly showering, eager to get a jump on her day.

Her cell showed several missed calls from Lyric, Syn and NeNe. Her voicemail was full, meaning the ladies had probably left her messages, telling her how stupid she was acting. Nope, she was most definitely not going to listen to them. Not today, thank you very much. "For fuckssake, grow up and quit being one of those people everyone hates," she muttered to her reflection in the mirror. The image staring back at her looked similar to her mother, with long black hair and almond shaped dark eyes, which pronounced their Japanese heritage. Jozlyn had asked why they'd not given her a traditional name like her mother Noriko. After hearing her father named her after his favorite aunt, it made her name all the more special.

Once she was dressed, she went to the back of her home, the space she used for relaxing. The cool floor beneath her feet didn't make a sound as she lowered herself into a sitting position. Meditation came easily for her as it was something she'd done with her mother since she'd been knee high to a grasshopper. Inhaling deeply, she focused her inner self, picturing the healing light she'd need throughout the day.

Twenty minutes later, Joz stood and stretched her arms above her head, going through a few yoga poses to complete her daily routine before she needed to grab something to eat and drink. The rumble of her stomach let her know she should have eaten before, but her mind and body conflicted sometimes.

She flicked the teapot on. While it boiled, she grabbed a box of cereal out of the cabinet, filled a bowl with her favorite guilty indulgence, and pulled the almond milk out of the fridge. By the time her tea was done, she had her breakfast on the counter. "Most definitely not the most balanced diet." She thought of the big man named Turo, and couldn't picture him eating what she whipped up. No, he was most assuredly a meat and eggs man in the morning and meat and potatoes the rest of the day. "And why do I care?" she groused.

Double checking her bag for her badge and keys, she made her way toward the front door, promising herself she'd make an effort to go out of her way to befriend the people she worked with. They were constantly inviting her to go out for drinks or parties. Next time, she'd go. Mind made up, she shut all thoughts of Turo, and the ladies she'd known forever, down.

At the hospital, she made her rounds, seeing patients and making notes in charts, eager to see Egypt. The little girl had made her feel more than she'd allowed others in her care to do. In her line of work, they'd been told not to get personally involved, but saying and doing were easier said than done, especially when you were staring in the tortured eyes of a child. She always got more personally involved than what most of her colleagues did, but she was still able to do her job without feeling as if she were crossing the line. This time wouldn't be any different.

Riding the elevator up to the psych ward, she made notes on her tablet about each of the patients she'd seen so far. The air on the fourth floor was heavy with a sense of wrongness. Her mother said she had a sixth sense about things. Of course, Joz never told anyone other than her mother about her intuitions, since others already thought she was odd.

"What's going on?" She asked Nichole, one of the nurses as she came to the desk.

"Where do I start? One of the patients attacked Leon, while another's dad tried to kill his kid last night."

Jozlyn's heart lodged in her throat. "Who? Who's dad?"

Nichole stared at her then looked down at the charts in front of her. "Oh, sorry, it was one of your patients actually, Ms. Light. She's fine, but he escaped before the cops got here. Sorry, I don't know much more than that."

"Thanks," she said, rushing toward Egypt's room. Lord, the child had to be scared. She paused outside the closed door, taking several deep breaths, trying to steady her nerves, knowing the child didn't need to see an adult who she was supposed to trust come in looking as freaked out as Joz felt. Feeling marginally more in control, she pushed the door open. The huddled figure on the bed didn't look anything like the fighting spitfire from the day before.

"He's going to kill me like he did my mama," Egypt promised, her voice quivering.

The words had Joz jolting to a halt. She'd thought the girl's mother had abandoned her. If the mother had been killed by the father then why was he not in jail?

"Hey, easy now. What happened?" As a professional, she needed facts.

"You can't keep me safe. Nobody can. My daddy would've killed me if I hadn't been able to scream loud enough." Egypt wouldn't look her in the eye.

Joz could see shivers wracking the frail frame of the little girl. Whoever her dad was, wherever he was, he needed to be caught.

Eyes like obsidian stared back at her. "You're a liar, just like my mommy. She left me with...I just want to die. Why won't you let me die, too?"

Her worry for Egypt trumped everything else as she sat down next to Egypt and forgot about protocol and procedures. Without hesitation, she wrapped her arms around Egypt, cradling her against her chest while the child cried. In her mind, she thought of fifty different ways she'd make Mr. Light pay for hurting his child. Being smart had its benefits, and one of them was never needing to look up facts on how to dispose of a body. Heck, she knew a family that owned a pig farm.

It seemed to take forever for Egypt to relax in her embrace. Even longer for her to realize she was safe. When she did, it appeared as if all the air was sucked out of her. "Take me away from here. Please," she begged.

"Sweetheart, I can't. Now that they know your father is dangerous, they'll take measures to ensure your safety." Jozlyn eased back, wanting to see if her words soothed or not.

A cynical laugh, much too old for one so young, rasped out. "Then go and don't come back. I probably won't be alive when you do anyhow. You don't know what you're dealing with. He's not normal…just go," Egypt cried, turning on her side.

She knew she couldn't leave without calling the aide to come sit with her, especially when the girl was raw from her recent attack and now what she probably deemed another betrayal. "I'm sorry, sweetheart, I promise you're safe here." Hollow words that only seemed to anger Egypt.

"Just go and don't come back," she screamed.

A guard came in, his hand on the tazer by his hip. "Everything okay in here, Dr. Rasey?"

The lump in her throat kept her from answering, but she nodded. As efficient and quickly as she could, she gathered her things. The aide would sit with her until shift change but wasn't allowed to speak to the patients. The knowledge didn't give Jozlyn any relief. "I'll stop in and see you before I leave," she promised.

Egypt kept her head turned toward the window with its closed blinds. Jozlyn thought of opening them, changing her mind at the last minute. With one last glance, she left the room, her heart in tatters. God, what had the father done to the mother, and how much had she seen, Jozlyn wondered?

"How is she doing?"

Jozlyn startled at the feminine voice. "Sheez, you scared the crap out of me, Tilly."

Tilly, an older, and by all accounts jaded, RN who had worked on the psychiatric floor for far too long, hated everyone, tried to look past Jozlyn into Egypt's room. Luckily the door had already shut. Jozlyn hated dealing with the older, bitter woman.

"She's upset. Are there notes on what happened exactly? How did her father get in?" Joz wanted answers.

"To be more pacific…he had an access badge just like a doctor and had the codes to all the doors.

He wore a doctor's lab coat, looked all professional, and everyone assumed he was a new doc on the floor. It wasn't until the patient began screaming like a banshee that one of the security guards went in. They thought she'd either tried to kill the good doc or tried to off herself again." Tilly shrugged.

The woman always said pacific instead of specific, making Jozlyn roll her eyes. She'd even tried to correct her, but Tilly had given her a blank stare as if she had no clue why Jozlyn was repeating a word. "Why didn't anyone question another doctor going into my patient's room?" Her mind began filing every nuance of Tilly's demeanor away. The woman was hiding something.

"Look, I don't have time to go over the ordeal. There's a report you'll get like everyone else," Tilly huffed, turning on her white sneakers and walked away.

Matilda, or Tilly to her friends, looked over her shoulder as she took a seat. Secretly, Jozlyn called her Matty the Mad Hatter but never to her face. There was something about her frizzy red hair that reminded her of Johnny Depp's rendition of the movie character. Her phone vibrated, the signal it was time for her to move to the next patient's room. Rolling her shoulders, she pulled the mental files she had on Aleria up, tucking Egypt away for now.

By the time she'd finished for the day and had her notes transcribed into the proper case files, the sun had set. "I feel like I've been wrung dry." She pulled her hair out of the low pony tail, raking her fingers through the heavy mass. Having it up all day had given her a low-grade headache, but she didn't want to deal with it down. Now, she quickly braided it off to the side, tying it off with a black band. Guilt swamped her as she looked at the clock and the fact she hadn't made it back up to Egypt's room. "Screw it. I'm her doctor, I make my own hours."

Not wanting to have to come back down to her office for her bag, she slung it over her shoulder, pocketing her office keys and making sure she locked up behind her. The halls were empty, since all of her colleagues already left for the night. "I'm the only moron with no life, clearly. And, I need to stop talking to myself," she muttered as she waited for the elevator.

Going through the steps of sliding her card through the security reader, she waited for the usual assent. When the doors opened onto the floor, the hairs on the back of her neck stood on end. Immediately she knew something wasn't right. Reaching into her bag, she pulled out her stun gun, holding it in front of her like it would protect her from anything and everything. For once, she kept her lips sealed as she eased around the corner.

The silence worried her. Usually there were two guards on duty, along with nurses and other personnel walking about or chatting as soon as she entered the hall, the noise always like static to her. Now, the lack thereof was almost deafening. A streak of red caught her eye. The trail looked as if someone had been bleeding and drug down the hall. God, it was like a bad B movie. She should get back on the elevator and call for help, but her body wouldn't obey. What if someone needed her help now?

A sound of breathing or gagging, near the nurses' desk where she'd seen the blood trail, froze Joz in her tracks. Taking a deep breath, she moved further down the hall, keeping her ears trained for anyone coming. The sight of a hand flopping out near her feet nearly made her squeal. Joz bent to inspect the body of the nurse it was attached to, finding a barely there pulse. Putting her finger up to her lips, Joz motioned for the woman not to make a sound. That was when Joz saw the chest wound. The gaping hole looked as if someone had tried to put their fist through her chest. Shit, she knew then the nurse wasn't going to make it. Tears leaked down Joz's cheeks as she looked into glassy green eyes, holding the woman's hand until her life faded away.

To the right of the nurses' station was Egypt's room. A blankness told her it was empty; that the little girl had somehow escaped before whoever had come in and killed at least one nurse. God, let it only be one. Her other patients' doors were securely locked, but the elevators were supposedly locked down as well with only emergency personnel able to access. Taking a deep breath, she made her way to check on Mick first. Her badge made a beep as she opened his door. The steady rise and fall of his chest showed he slept peacefully, probably from his nightly dose of sleep meds. Looking both ways down the hallway, she eased next door to Aleria's room, praying she too slept. The imperceptible beep echoed loudly down the corridor or at least to Joz's ears.

"Sssh, he'll hear you and come back," Aleria whispered, glancing around the room.

"Who?" Joz asked.

"The monster." Aleria swallowed then pointed toward the window. "A little girl went out there."

Trying to follow the ramblings of a young woman who wasn't crazy, yet her words didn't register for several long seconds. "What child?"

Aleria blinked slowly, licked her lips as if she was thinking. "She looks young, but not too young.

Dark hair and eyes. Maybe mixed heritage, but I couldn't say for sure. She was outside my window for only a moment. I know you think I'm crazy," Aleria paused, her eyes darting back to the door. "The monster came in too, but I pretended to sleep. He banged on the window when he saw the girl then ran back out when the window wouldn't give. I think he would've killed me if he'd realized I saw him. You have to get me out of here. He has a way in and out like you do."

"I'm calling security. We need to lock the hospital down. I need to find Egypt," she tried to reassure Aleria as she moved back toward the door.

"Don't leave me. What if he comes back?" Her fear wasn't unfounded.

She looked out the crack in the door, making sure it was clear before pulling the cell out of her purse. "Fuck, do I call 911 or security?" Figuring the cops would take longer, she dialed the number they all had for the security office. In the wing they were in, surely there was at least someone with a gun near.

"This is Dr. Rasey. I have a dead nurse and a patient missing while the perpetrator is on the loose." She gave her location and answered details before tossing her phone back in her bag. Protocol would go into effect, locking everyone inside or outside within moments. She didn't want to be locked inside a patient's room, not when Egypt was possibly outside alone. "They'll lock everything down. Nobody can get in or out even with a passkey like mine. You'll be safe," she told Aleria, hoping she was telling the truth.

Chapter Four

Jozlyn eased out the door again, worried if she didn't hurry she'd be screwed. Once Aleria's door locked behind her, she hurried to the exit at the end of the hall near the stairs. Every floor had a fire escape. How the hell had Egypt gotten outside? She didn't stop to think of the how's only knew she needed to be outside as well. Her damn mother's words echoed in her head from long ago. *"One day, you'll hear a buzz inside you. Don't ignore it. Follow where it leads, for it will lead to your destiny."* The buzzing was like a swarm of bees all ganging up on her brain any time she turned in a direction they didn't want her going. Finally, as she reached the basement level, the hum quieted as did everything else.

"Okay, where to now?" Her heart thudded against her ribs. Row after row of cars was all she saw. The buzzing started again as she stood there, making the decision she needed to move all the clearer. One foot in front of the other, she kept to the shadows, looking around wishing she could call out for Egypt.

Scraping to her left near the exit ramp had her swallowing. Her tazer gave her little comfort, but she held it in front of her with her purse slung over her chest, thankful she'd used the crossbody bag lately. Tucked between the wall and the last car, she noticed what appeared to be a hospital gown. "Egypt?" she called out.

When nobody answered she moved closer. "Sweetheart, it's me, Dr. Rasey. Are you okay?" She looked around the darkened corner. "Oh, God, please be okay. I don't think I can handle it if...no, she's fine," Jozlyn muttered.

A sniff and then a shuffle reached her before a dark head peered around the fender of the vehicle. "He's here. We must hide." Her head whipped back and forth.

Jozlyn wasn't sure who he was; if the monster was the same as Egypt's dad, but at that moment she wasn't taking any chances. "Egypt, come with me. We can't stay here. If he's looking for you, he'll find you like I did." In fact, she wondered why he hadn't.

"I hurt him, too. Now, I don't know what to do or where to go. My mommy was supposed to protect me." Her voice quivered.

The banging of the door at the end of the garage made her jump. "Let's go. We need to hurry." Grabbing the hand that Egypt lifted up, Joz knew her life was never going to be the same. Of course, they had to live through the night. Whatever was searching for them growled. The sound inhuman and angry.

Her little VW wasn't parked in the underground lot, which she was damn glad as they raced toward the outside. She calculated the distance between where they were and where she'd parked, figuring it was within twenty feet. If luck was on their side, they'd make it before whatever was in the garage noticed they weren't there any longer.

Egypt gripped her fingers in a vice like grip, running next to her like a sprinter. As they hit the lot, she wished for the first time she had a new car with one of the auto unlock options. Her hands shook as she tried to insert the key in the hole, finally getting it in and had Egypt crawl into the passenger seat. Each second was like a lifetime as she was sure whatever was coming after them wasn't going to give up, and he or it wasn't human. Why she thought it, she wasn't sure, but once it popped into her mind, it wouldn't leave. Next, she was the one who would need therapy.

"I can just imagine what my therapist is gonna say." She looked in the rearview mirror as she exited the hospital lot. "Hell, I just absconded with a patient from a psych ward. I'm pretty sure I just broke several laws." Clenching the steering wheel so tightly her knuckles turned white, Joz couldn't believe what she'd done. She had no clue what she was going to do or where she was going to go. The only people she knew who were somewhat shady were the Iron Wolves MC. Sure, Lyric and Syn said they weren't a bad biker club, but her friends also were really quick to suggest they hang out somewhere else. They also never let her sleep over at their houses. All that surely meant they might have an idea of what she should do or where she could go.

Mind made up, she drove to the place she'd thought she would never go back to. A place she'd fantasized about, but never gotten to see inside of. Well, out of the pan and into the fire.

"Buckle up, Egypt." She pulled her own seatbelt on now that they were away from the hospital and had a clear direction.

"Where're we going, Dr. Rasey?" Big brown eyes stared at her from the passenger seat.

"Call me Jozlyn. We're going to go see if some friends of mine can help us." Heck, if nothing else it's a safe place to call the police. Surely, they'd understand why she'd taken off with Egypt Light. Traumatic stress she'd claim.

The club's big iron gates were open with the lot full of trucks, bikes, and a few cars. Syn's big beast was near the back with a spot next to it. Her hands shook as she maneuvered in beside it.

"Okay, we're going to go and talk to my friends. I need you to…crap, you need something else to put on." In the back, her gym bag had a pair of yoga pants and a T-shirt in it that was clean since she hadn't been to the gym that day. "Here, slip these on. They'll be way too big for you, but they'll be better than that gown."

Egypt, love her, hastily put the clothing on then gave the thumbs up sign. What had the little girl seen in her short life that what had occurred tonight, didn't seem to freak her out nearly as much, as it did Joz? "You're really a brave little nugget, you know that right?" Joz asked with her hand on the door handle.

In the dark interior, Egypt blinked. "So are you."

Taking a deep breath, she shoved open her door. "Let's go."

Turo smelled her long before he saw her. His wolf stood up and growled, wanting to claim their mate. After Jenna had done her thing on the poor broken woman, she'd blinked them all back to the Iron Wolves. So much for him taking some time away. Now, his wolf raked at his skull, itching along his skin. Instead, he stayed behind the bar, arms crossed and waited. For what he didn't know, but then another scent hit him as the door opened.

He leapt over the bar in a flash, startling the few wolves sitting there. He heard Kellen say something, was sure it had something to do about humans, but zero fucks were given as he locked onto the miniature version of the woman he'd saved next to Jozlyn. Goddess, thinking her name gave him a semi-hard-on.

"Who are you?" he asked as he got down on one knee, keeping his tone low and soothing, knowing a startled deer when he saw one, and this child was ready to flee, just as surely as any startled animal.

Jozlyn placed herself in front of him. "Hello, Arturo. Is Lyric or Syn around? This is my niece, and well...I just wanted to ask them a favor."

He inhaled deeply, looking up at his unclaimed mate. Even on one knee he was almost eye-to-eye with the woman. "First off, the girls aren't in tonight. Second, don't lie to me, hahai, or I'll tan that fine ass red. Now, let's start over, shall we?" He gave the little girl he knew was the daughter of the woman sleeping in the clinic a smile. He hoped it would reassure her. "What's your name, little one?"

"Egypt Rose Light, Arturo, and you're kinda scary," she answered him.

Laughing, he patted her on the head. "Well, Egypt, I know your mama, Asia." He watched recognition light the dark eyes then tears well in them. "Hey, now, no crying. Your mama wouldn't like that."

"My mama…is…dead," she cried, turning her head into his unclaimed mate's side.

Turo looked at Jozlyn and winced. Her dark eyes were spitting bullets at him. If she'd had a gun, he was sure she'd have shot him right then and there. Of course, he'd have recovered. It would've just hurt a bit. "Honey, your mama isn't...she's here, but she's pretty tired. Do you want to go see her?"

"What's going on, Turo?" Kellen's voice thundered behind him.

"This little bit is Asia's daughter, and this is Jozlyn." He faced his alpha, meeting Kellen's gaze with a steady stare.

The mental link opened. *"Why the fuck is there a kid in my club, and why haven't you claimed your mate?"*

Turo snorted. *"Hello pot said the kettle. How long did you wait to claim your mate? Besides, she's too young, human, and too...everything for the likes of me."*

Kellen's bright blue eyes flashed. *"Is this the reason you were leaving the pack?"*

He owed it to Kellen to be honest with him. With a nod, he didn't make excuses, just left it at a nod and held his ground. Kellen may be the alpha, the Iron Wolf, but Turo was not a young pup. He chose to be part of the Iron Wolves. He'd been drawn here. Now he knew why and couldn't claim his fated mate. Fucking-A fates suck.

"*I'll eliminate the reason and then you can stay.*" Kellen took a menacing step forward.

"*Touch one hair on her head, and there will be a war unlike any you've ever seen,*" he promised, his words coming out low and even through their link.

"*That's what I thought. You'll be mated and claiming before too long, my friend. Now, back to my original question. What's doing with kids and unclaimed mates in my club?*" He placed his fists on his hips as if Turo hadn't just threatened him.

Turo shook his head. Kellen was almost as batshit crazy as the Fey Queen.

"Well hello, did someone just say my name?" Jenna asked from behind him.

He blinked, wondering if the other being was reading his mind. She tapped her temple and smiled. With a grin of his own, he slammed walls in place, making her wince.

"Dang, son, that was mean. Now, aren't you just the spitting image of your mother. I'm sure you hear that all the time. Tsk, tsk, who thought it was okay to bring a little girl into a bar?" Jenna pinned Jozlyn with her turquoise gaze. "Oh, aren't you just lovely. Come along, we'll chat and get to know each other. You meet my bestie Kellen?" Jenna leaned in toward Jozlyn and Egypt. "He only growls really loudly, but he's a big softie. Aren't you? Yes, you are. Oh yes, you are," she cooed as if she were talking to a little kid or a favorite pet.

It took all of Turo's self-control not to burst out laughing as Kellen's head fell forward, his chin resting on his chest as he muttered *must not kill the Fey* over and over in a growled whisper.

"Kellen, I'll check on Team Styles while I'm here as well, might as well get r done in one fell swoop." Jenna tossed her long blonde hair over her shoulder, grabbing onto one of Egypt's hands and then Jozlyn's.

He took a step to follow, pulling up short as Kellen moved into his path. "We need to talk," Kellen said.

Damn, he didn't want to get into a pissing contest with his alpha. Hell, he'd called the man and asked for his help. Now, it looked as though any thought of leaving the pack had just flown, or in this case, walked in the door with a tiny stranger in tow. Yeah, fate sure had a funny way of slapping you in the face when you least expected it.

"I can see the wheels spinning in that monster brain of yours. Let's have a sit down in my office. I keep the good shit there." Kellen's stride didn't falter as he headed toward his sanctuary in the club.

Turo shook his head and then he followed, knowing it was no use to not do as instructed. Kellen would just come find him. Not that he was scared of the Iron Wolf. Of course, the fact the other man could shift into a beast of myth most hadn't truly believed in until recently, but Turo had also learned much in his years. A lesson learned was, that you didn't turn down an opportunity to gain important information.

"Want one?" Kellen held up a bottle of Makers.

"Absolutely," Turo agreed.

Once he had two full glasses, Kellen made his way over to his recliner, handed Turo his glass then sat. "Alright, I'm sure you're wondering if Jenna has shared anything with me about our mystery woman. Well, the answer is no. However, I need to ask you a few things. First and foremost, what the fuck is going on with you? I knew when you came here there was something different about you, but I wasn't sure what it was. Now, I'm thinking I should've told my father to ask more pointed questions. As the alpha, I'm asking. What's up with you? And don't feed me no bullshit line. Where did you come from? What are your origins? I took you as a straight up lone wolf, but I think there's more to you than that. Where's your original pack?"

Turo looked at the amber liquid, hearing the questions fired at him like bullets from a gun. He'd guessed Kellen would want to know what was what when it came to him. However, he wasn't sure how much to tell. Taking a long sip, he met the piercing blue gaze of the alpha. "My name is Arturo Anoa'i. I was originally from New Zealand, but my family moved around quite a bit back in the day. When I didn't find my true mate, I left my pack to search for her. I've been searching for hundreds of years." He watched Kellen's face to see how his words would affect the alpha.

Shock rolled off Kellen in waves. "Holy shit. So, you're telling me you're what…a couple hundred years old?"

Shrugging, Turo saw no reason to be completely honest. "I stopped counting birthdays after three hundred. It's been a few decades since I saw my three hundredth birthday."

Kellen slammed the rest of his drink before he spoke again. "Damn, you're an old motherfucker."

"Yeah, I guess you could say that. However, there's still life in this old dude." He tapped his chest. "I don't know why I'm still kicking when most of my pack, if not all of my former pack, has all died. I've gone back but could never find them. I assume they've all joined the Goddess." No longer did the loss of his family hurt like it had centuries ago. Hell, even fifteen years ago, until he'd found the Iron Wolves, he'd felt the ache of loss.

"Then why were you leaving us?" Kellen stood and went to refill his drink.

Turo sighed, thinking of the tiny human named Jozlyn. His unclaimed mate. "You saw her. She's too fragile for the likes of me. Too young, and fuck all if I'm worthy of the likes of her."

Kellen slammed the bottle on top of the bar. "What the hell are you talking about? You're one of the best men, not to mention wolves, I know. I'd trust you with my mate's life. That human is your mate. She was created for you. The Goddess knows what she's doing. You fuck it up, and you're a dumbass who's too stupid to live, like one of those heroines my mate is always cursing in books." He sloshed more of his favorite drink into his glass, holding up the bottle.

With a shake of his head, Turo sipped at his drink, feeling the burn as it went down to his stomach. "I'm gonna go check on them. Can't make any hasty decisions today anyhow."

"Don't be a dumbass, Turo. You fuck around too long you could lose the best thing in your life. Trust me, son, you don't want to do that."

He laughed. Hearing Kellen call him son always amused him.

Kellen raised his middle finger. "Should I start calling you old man?"

"Seems more appropriate, but others might get suspicious. Right now, I'd like to keep my secrets between us. No need to freak the other guys out."

"Xan's my second, which means he needs to know what's going on in case I'm incapacitated. Don't worry, the man knows how to keep pack business between us. Trust me, he's every bit as much in control as me, without the title." Kellen scrunched up his brows. "Jenna said the woman is waking, let's go."

Chapter Five

Turo and Kellen beat feet to the clinic at the back of the club, going out the door through the private entrance of his office, so they didn't need to go through the bar. Worry for Jozlyn and the child she'd brought had him at a near run. He opened his senses as they hit the parking lot, scanning for any threat. The scents of gasoline and air mixed with shifter and humans hit him. He filtered them through his mind, cataloguing them, while he made his way to the hidden entrance to the clinic. Kellen had become obsessed with safety after the attack on the club, making he and his wolf glad for the extra protection now that his almost mate was on the premises.

Kellen reached the entrance first, using the new retinal scanner Rowan, their newest member who was mated to Lyric, had installed. The former Navy SEAL had all kinds of security tips and protocols he was working to add to their homes and businesses.

Breezy, mate to Xan, sat at a desk near the opened door, her blonde hair pulled back in a ponytail with its pink and purple streaks playing peekaboo occasionally. She smiled at Kellen and Turo. "Hey, alpha, Turo. Second door on the right. Try to tone down the alphaness," she instructed.

"Sure, I'll get right on that. Xan perfect it yet?" Kellen asked.

She laughed. "Right. Xan Mother-Fucking Carmichael is still a work in progress." She winked then went back to looking at the computer screen.

Turo walked around Kellen, his wolf on high alert. Telling the beast to pull back was like telling the tide to stop.

At the door to the room, he heard voices murmuring. A soft young voice, followed by Asia's. The one he was searching for wasn't talking, but he could feel her like a lover's caress washing over him. His entire body tensed. Hell, he was hard as stone, not something an impressionable child needed to see. Adjusting himself, he worked to get control of his raging hard-on, back to some semblance of *not so noticeable*, before walking in.

Three sets of brown eyes turned toward him while one set of turquoise gave him a slow blinking appraisal. He suppressed a shudder as he felt her digging too deep. "Get out of my mind, Fey," he growled.

"Be nice," Jenna admonished. "Not in front of the children." She wagged a finger at him, smiling as she stroked her hand over Asia's brow.

"She's not crazy, is she?" Asia asked Turo.

He shook his head. "I'm afraid I think she invented it, therefore it makes her…not."

Jenna tilted her head. "I think you just insulted me or complimented. You," she pointed at Jozlyn. "Which is it?"

Joz looked frightened, and considering the fact she was in a room full of shifters, that was understandable. "Um, I think he was saying you're really great."

"Pfft, he has you blown already." Jenna started making the sound of a fake laser gun, something he was sure he'd heard on a kid's game in rapid fire as she held her fingers up like they were a gun.

"Um, Jenna, can you turn the crazy down? Or, better yet, since we have a doctor here who specializes in crazy, maybe she can tranq you or something. What say you, doc, you got a shot you can give crazy maker here?" Kellen asked coming into the room.

Jenna narrowed her eyes. "You realize I have a straight pathway to your little team, right? I mean, they love auntie Jennaveve so hard they may petition to live in my realm." She sniffed and left the room.

"Jennaveve," Kellen roared making the windows rattle.

Jozlyn looked from the door to Turo, back to the door again. "What the heck is going on?"

Egypt held her mother's hand. "Mommy, I want to go home."

Turo looked up to the ceiling, wondering how the hell he'd become the keeper of sane. "Alright, listen up ladies. It seems I am the voice of reason and well shit, pardon my french, but this is the safest place for all of you right now. Joz, I know you're probably freaked out, which is putting it mildly, I'm sure. However, you can't leave at this time. Asia, Egypt, you both know what kind of danger awaits outside this compound. Asia, I think you have some explaining to do with your little one here. I'm gonna take Jozlyn here for a little walk while you do that. If you need anything just holler, or whatever they told you before." Shit, he didn't know what they did here at the clinic, if they had buzzers or what.

"What did she mean by having her blown?" Egypt asked.

Jozlyn looked puzzled then laughed. "She meant he had me...believing everything he says."

"Oh," Egypt said, then narrowed her eyes. "That's not wise. You shouldn't do that. A fool is born every minute of every day. You don't want to be one of them, do you?"

A wry chuckle escaped Turo. "You are one smart little girl, Egypt. And to answer your question, no, Joz is far from a fool. I'm pretty sure her bull...crap meter has gone crazy since meeting me." He met Jozlyn's dark stare with his own. Goddess, he could get lost in her gaze, could imagine waking up to it every morning. The last thought had him shuttering his thoughts and eyes.

"I'm going to check in with Kellen then I'll come back for you, Joz. You three be good." He left before he could make a fool of himself and kiss the hurt look off of Joz's face. Fuck, he was becoming a damn pussy like the other wolves.

Joz wasn't sure what the heck was going on, but she felt as though she'd stepped into the Twilight Zone. Not to mention, she'd willingly brought herself and Egypt to them. There was something about the woman, Jenna, or Jennaveve, something other-worldly.

"You have questions?" Asia asked, looking better than even moments before.

She swallowed. "I don't think I want to voice what's in my head. What's the saying? Ignorance is bliss." Yep, she was going with that.

A scream coming from the hallway had her moving in front of the bed, putting her body in front of mother and child. "Stay calm. I'll get us out of here." Joz wasn't sure where she'd take them, or how she'd get them out, but she'd do it.

Asia laughed. "Sweet child, you are too precious for words. Egypt, can you do me a favor and go get that big man named Turo. Tell him to get his cowardly ass back in here."

Jozlyn didn't like anyone talking about...she didn't allow herself to continue her train of thoughts. Turo wasn't her anything, and never would be, no matter how much she wished it. And yes, she'd wished it more than a dozen times since she'd laid eyes on him.

Egypt shook her head. "No mama, I don't want to leave you."

Asia opened her mouth at the same time the door banged open, allowing Turo to enter with a look of terror on his face. Immediately Jozlyn went to him. "What is it?"

"Babies," he muttered.

Jozlyn, uncomprehending what the heck he was talking about waited. When it didn't appear as if he was going to say any more, she tugged on the T-shirt that was snug enough on his body it showcased each and every muscle on his stomach and his pecs.

"Turo, focus. What do babies and screaming have to do with you looking like…well, like you were just kicked in the groin by a horse?" she asked. Then exasperated when he still didn't take his eyes away from the door, she pinched his side. "Damn, do you not have an ounce of fat on you?"

He shook his head. "What the hell…err, heck are you talking about?"

She glared up at him. "There was screaming, then you came in muttering about babies. What the heck is going on?"

A grin split his gorgeous features. "Laikyn is in labor. With babies. You should see Kellen. I think he passed out at the first scream," he laughed.

Risking a glance toward the woman and child, she couldn't help but smile. Never would she have imagined this huge warrior so excited by the prospect of his boss passing out. Of course, she'd only met the intimidating man named Kellen a handful of times. To say he was a very macho man would be putting it lightly. "Shouldn't you be there making sure he doesn't need help? You know, in case he does fall down." Kellen was almost as big as Turo. She couldn't imagine one of the men back at the hospital being the ones to lift him onto a gurney if he'd passed out on them.

"Nah, he'll be fine. Jenna's got him."

The sound of feet pounding down the hall had Turo stepping out, giving her a chance to see Lyric and her fiancé rushing by. A few days prior and she'd have rushed out to say hi, now she felt like an intruder. Gah, she hated not knowing where she belonged in her friends lives. Once she became part of their circle, she was sure she'd always have a place. Now, something had shifted, and she didn't like it one bit.

"Come here, child. You need to let the wolves take care of their own," Asia said.

Turo growled, making Asia and Egypt both jump.

"Hey, back off, buddy. What's up with that rumbling nonsense?" Jozlyn asked, poking her finger into Turo's rock-hard abs. "Jesus, what do you do, a thousand sit-ups a day?"

"Not quite, hahai," he said, grabbing her finger and lifted it to his mouth.

Once his lips touched her finger, butterflies took flight in her stomach. She'd read about the sensation in some of her romance novels, had heard friends talk about having those type of feelings toward men, but she'd never experienced them herself until now.

"Butterfly," she murmured while looking into his mesmerizing gaze.

"You are as beautiful as one. How did you know what I called you?" He asked, holding onto her finger.

Her heart thudded against her rib cage. "I speak several languages." She shrugged. Languages came easily to her as did most things once she read them or saw them.

He nodded, opened his mouth, but stopped as the sound of Laikyn cursing pierced the air.

"Yo, Turo, we might need you to come and do your bouncing thing," a man yelled.

She raised her brows, wondering exactly what the man did other than bartend.

"I can see you have questions. Promise not to run, and I'll answer them all. I will answer them," he stressed looking at the bed then back at Jozlyn.

Asia nodded, holding Egypt close to her.

More cursing and the sound of thuds had Turo moving toward the door. "Listen, I need you three to stay put. I'll be back shortly."

Turo rushed out the door, when all he wanted was to pull the tiny form of his mate into his arms and never let her go. Shit, his alpha's mate picked a fine time to go into labor. Chuckling, he rushed down the hall, coming to a hard stop at the sight that met his eyes.

Kellen sprawled beneath Xan and Rowan, fighting with all his might to get up. "What the ever-loving fuck is going on?" He let his wolf surface, the beast that was hundreds of years old, not just the one they saw normally, but the alpha who was more than capable of putting them all in their place.

Xan turned, bright blue eyes blazing. "He's ready to rip into everyone who is trying to help

Laikyn deliver his kids. Now, you gonna help us, or do we add you to our woopass pile?" he growled.

"Ah, puppy, don't tug this tail. You don't want to bite off more than you can chew." Turo flicked his gaze at the closed door then back at Kellen. "Where's Jenna?"

"I'm right here, geez. Simmer down, boys. Let big boy up. He'll be fine now," Jenna ordered. Next to her stood a pink haired pixie with glowing violet eyes.

"You think that's wise?" Xan asked, his body heaving as he held Kellen down.

"I will fucking gut your asses, if you don't let me go," Kellen said in a low voice.

"Now, now, wolfie, you need to chill. Your mate in there is not in the mood for these antics. I had to get my girl here to help me since Team Kellen is coming. You ready?" Jenna held her hand down for him to take.

Turo wasn't sure what the hell he expected, but Kellen nodding and shoving Xan along with Rowan off like they weighed nothing wasn't it. "Were y'all just playing a little game of slap and tickle or what?" he asked as Kellen dusted off his hands.

"Seriously, you are not right in the head, old wolfie," Jenna muttered. "Come, Kellen, you can kick his ass later."

Kellen got in Turo's face. "Slap and tickle? If my kids weren't ready to rip my mate in half, I'd show you how I play slap and tickle."

"Nah, I'm good. I prefer playing hide and seek. We can play that when you finish," he growled.

The alpha stopped with one hand on the door. "You are not leaving this pack. Once pack, always pack. Feel me?" His alpha stare pinned Turo with a laser like focus.

"Go see to your family, Kellen. I'll be here when Team Kellen comes. I got money on how many arrive. My number is four." Turo took a sick sort of pleasure at the instant drain of color from Kellen's face.

"Don't even joke, man."

Rowan slapped him on the back. "I got money on three. One boy and two girls. My Harlow needs a couple playmates, and someone to look out for them all."

Xan crossed his arms. "I say a boy and a girl. An even balance."

Chapter Six

Kellen felt sweat rolling down his back as he stepped into the room they'd created for the birth of his and Laikyn's babies. Shit, just saying babies had his gut twisting. Where the hell was his favorite whiskey when he needed a shot or ten? He wiped the back of his hand across his mouth before stepping next to the bed.

"Did you get your shit calm?" Laikyn asked.

He grabbed her hand. "Yeah, sorry about that. I just needed to do something, and seeing you in pain sort of freaked me out." Her face grimaced then she squeezed his fingers in a vice like grip.

Once she finished panting, she smiled. "Ya think? I need you to be here for me and the babies, not freaking the fuck out every time I scream. Because newsflash, I'm gonna scream a few times more I think."

"Not while mama Jenna is here. Now, let's see what we have going on." The Fey Queen began moving around the room, before coming to stand at the foot of the bed. "Lula, can you stand at the head of the bed and place both hands on Laikyn's temples? I want you to send soothing thoughts through her so the babies know they're safe."

"Excuse me, but who the fuck is Lula?" Kellen moved to intercept Lula before she could touch any part of his mate.

"Kellen Styles, meet Lula the dragonrex, who you've already met, only now she's in her human form. Now, get the hell next to your mate, or so help me, I'll send you to visit Creed. I can guarantee you, he'll not be pleased to have a visitor right now."

"You're *the* Lula?" Kellen asked in an awed whisper.

"Why so shocked? You're a shifter, yet you think I can't be?" Lula's voice was a husky mixture of feminine youth and something other worldly. It had Kellen moving back next to his mate.

"How you feeling?" If Laikyn said one thing felt off, he'd kick the dragonrex shifter to the hall; Jenna be damned.

Laikyn smiled. "Much better. Whatever you're doing, keep doing it."

Lula smiled. "If I can touch you, it'll be better. The babies remember me from when you visited our realm. And don't give me that look, wolfie. I can and will kick your ass," Lula growled.

He refrained from saying another word. *"If at any time you need me to go all wolfie on any one's ass, you tell me, and dragonrex kicking my ass or not, I'll do it."* He promised Laikyn through their link.

"All right, team, I think the first one is ready to make an appearance. Xan," she yelled. "Where's your mate?"

Breezy came strolling in with two small baby things he had no clue what they were called, only knew that once his kids came out they'd go into one of them. That was if he allowed them out of his arms. Goddess, he couldn't wait to hold his children.

"Oh, I feel pressure, Jenna," Laikyn moaned.

"Good, push with it. I can't take it all away, but the worst should be gone. Come on, Lake, push harder," Jenna ordered.

Kellen felt like the world was standing still as Laikyn grunted and pushed, her fingers biting into his where he held one, the other held the bar of the bed. Luckily for them, they'd had reinforced stainless-steel bars made for the shifter patients, unknowing they'd have a mama delivering. One who could bend regular poles.

Just as he began to fear she couldn't do it, Jenna cheered, and then held up a dark haired red-faced baby. She waved her hand, and then, the child let loose a wail that had him grinning.

"Congratulations, it's a boy. Okay, folks. Here comes baby number two. Breezy, can you take care of this gorgeous little guy?" Jenna passed his son off to Xan's mate.

He was torn, wanting to see his first born and being there for his mate. Being there for Laikyn won out as she held his hand tighter, and then, his second child came out, crying without Jenna's help.

"Wow, impatient little guy," Kellen marveled as Jenna waved her hand over the dark-haired boy.

"Twins, you have what looks like identical twin boys, Kellen. Oh, wait. Breezy, can you put this one next to his brother. Looks like mama has another surprise for us. Keep pushing Laikyn, I know you're tired, hun. Come on, you can do it."

"Oh, Goddess, triplets," Laikyn wheezed.

"You're doing great," Kellen whispered. He brushed his lips over her forehead and watched as Jenna lifted his third child up.

"Congratulations, papa, it's a girl."

"Oh, I still feel like I need to push. Jenna, how many babies are in there?" Laikyn wailed looking frightened.

Breezy took the third child. His third child, while his mate began to look panicked. "Mon Chaton, one, two, or ten, we'll love them all. You're incredible."

His mate glared at him. "One and done. One and done, Kellen Styles. No more fucking in Fey. Ever."

Jenna laughed. "Come on, this one needs a little more to come out."

In seconds that seemed like hours, another dark-haired angel appeared. "You're doing great, Laikyn." Kellen felt like he'd just battled a horde of rogue wolves and came out with his ass handed to him.

"Another girl. Wow, that's two for two," Jenna said with awe lacing her tone.

"They're just beautiful. I mean, truly, beautiful," Breezy whispered.

Kellen looked down at his mate. "How're you feeling? Any more in there?"

Tears flowed from her eyes. "Four babies. Kellen, we have four little Styles."

He brushed the tears from her cheeks. "We'll be fine. You're going to be a great mama. I can't wait to tell Syn and Bodhi."

"Of course, we are. I mean, you're Kellen and…oh," she yelped.

"Sorry, I had to finish cleaning you up and getting all the other business down here done. You know it's not all magic and stuff." Jenna dusted her hands off.

Kellen looked down, amazed to see Jenna had cleansed everything away as if nothing had happened. He'd been to births before and knew from experience they could be messy and sometimes downright gory. However, his mate didn't look like a woman who'd just delivered four large babies. And yes, he was sure they were big and not just because they were his.

"Breezy, can I bring them over to Laikyn to hold?" It seemed odd to be asking when he was the alpha, but he wasn't the expert in this situation.

"Um, yeah, sure. Do you have names for these gorgeous little ones?" Breezy pushed the two carriers over. Each one held two babies.

"Holy shit, I've got a set of twin girls and a set of twin boys." Kellen wasn't sure what was happening but looking down at the perfect little faces, had everything spinning.

"Man down. Wolf down. Beep, beep, beep," he heard Jenna yelling as he felt something hard hit him in the head.

Turo rushed into the room at the sound of Jenna yelling, to find Kellen lying flat on the ground. He was pushed aside as Bodhi and Syn made their way into the room, looks of awe and...did Bodhi have his phone out taking pics of their alpha passed out? Shit, that man had a death wish or something.

He looked around the room, opening his senses for the threat, his wolf ready to protect his pack. Nails became claws and his sight enhanced, looking for anything he didn't consider friend. "What the hell happened?" he asked.

"He passed out. I think he's a little overwhelmed. Come on, big guy, wakey-wakey," Jenna said, slapping Kellen on the cheeks.

Laikyn stared over the side of the bed, a look of horror on her face. "Is he okay?"

"Yep, he just took a diver," Lula agreed.

"I can't believe my brother passed the eff out. That has got to be one for the books. By the way, I in no way approved my mate taking and uploading pics of my brother just now," Syn laughed.

"If someone would have told me the big bad alpha would pass out over the birth of his...whoa, how many did you give him, Lake?" Turo peered over the little things holding the babies.

Laikyn held up four fingers. "Two boys and two girls. Go Team Kellen." Her smile lit up her face.

Bodhi held his phone up. "Hey, it's not my fault he presented me with YouTube gold."

A growl escaped Laikyn. "Bodhi, you delete that right now, or so help me, I'll make it to where you can't fuck for six months."

Syn giggled, then covered her man's groin area. "That is just mean. I like how you think, if you weren't...you know, threatening my pleasure stick."

"Oh god, you do not call his dick that do you?" Breezy rolled her eyes.

Bodhi grinned. "Hey, all I can say is I'm that good."

"Whoop," Turo yelled, rousing Kellen from the ground. "I won. I said you were having quads, and damned if I wasn't right. Shit, that's like one in a few million. Congrats, Kellen and Laikyn."

Kellen climbed to his feet, rubbing the back of his head. "Fucking-A, what the hell happened?"

Laikyn laughed. "In Lula's words…you took a diver."

Kellen glared at the pink haired pixie. "This does not leave the room. Hear me?"

Jenna typed on a hand-held device. "Oops, I already put it on Fey Board. Sorry," she mumbled.

"What the hell is Fey Board?" He growled.

"Like a chat room for Fey," she announced, then moved to the other side of the bed. "I'm kidding. Geez, lighten up, wolfie. Besides, your friend over there was the one threatening to put it on YouTube. Now, my duty is done. I must go. Things to do, things to blow up and all. I'll be back to visit my godchildren in a day or so." She placed a kiss on each of their foreheads, a glow shimmering around her and them.

Kellen growled at Bodhi. "Boy, I'll make it to where you never have any babies of your own." His eyes flashed a bright blue.

Bodhi held up his hands. "Done deleted."

Turo cleared his voice. "Congrats, Kellen, Laikyn. Um, you got names for…all these little ones?" Holy shit, four babies. He couldn't wrap his head around having one baby, let alone four. His gaze swept over the tiny woman lying with a serene smile on her face and wondered how she carried four of the big bad alpha's kids at once.

"Ancient Feynese secret," Jenna laughed into his mind.

"Dammit, Fey, get out of my head," he growled.

"Err, Turo, you okay, man?" Kellen looked up from touching one of the infants in the baby holder.

Placing a finger to his temple. "Your bestie decided to pop into my head."

Kellen tilted his head in a wolfish way. "She's pretty adept at doing that from time to time. Best to just let her in; otherwise, you'll just get a migraine, and I don't mean her." He winced as if something pained him. "Fucking, Jennaveve, I was only kidding. Damn Fey can't take a joke."

Laikyn held out her arms. "Hand me my babies."

A mother's orders were never to be denied. However, Kellen looked frightened. "Breezy, a little help here?"

"Oh, you big scaredy cat." Xan's mate, Breezy lifted one of the babies with a pink cap on her head and handed her to Laikyn followed by the other little girl. "What's their names?" she asked.

Turo rocked back on his feet wondering what he should do, or if he should leave. He felt as if he was intruding on a private moment between them and their immediate family. A knock on the door saved him from doing or saying something stupid, giving him an opportunity to make an exit.

"We had a couple names for a girl and boy picked out," Laikyn said looking down at her baby girls. "Everleigh Rose and Enzley Rebel. Leigh is after Kellen's mother. We sort of thought we could use it in a couple different spellings if we had twin girls. Rose is after my mother and Rebel is after Jennaveve."

Breezy pushed a chair behind Kellen. "Sit, alpha, so you can cuddle your boys."

He stopped with one foot out the door to watch Kellen take two tiny bundles wrapped in blue into his massive tattooed arms. With great care, Breezy showed the big man how to hold them properly. Turo would have laughed at the true fear on Kellen's face, except the moment was too poignant to interrupt. "What's their names gonna be?" he asked.

Kellen didn't look up from his kids, smiling as he spoke. "Jaggar Oneil and Jaxon Xander. Although I wanted to pronounce Jagger as Yager, but Laikyn put her foot down. She said no way was she having a kid named after an alcoholic drink."

"Oh my," Breezy whispered. "Does Xan know?"

Kellen lifted his head. "He does now."

Standing in the entryway was Xan, a smile almost as bright as Kellen's on his face. "Kids got a great name, Jaggar's not too bad either."

Kellen put the babies back into the cradle. "Ha, my kid isn't going to be referred to as Xander Freaking anything," Kellen growled. "Besides, I figured since you're clearly still trying to figure out how to make babies, what with you still *practicing*." He made air quotes before continuing. "While I clearly know how to get r done in one fell swoop, with not just one or two but four healthy bundles of joy, the least I could do is name one after you."

"Wow, really, you might want to dial back on the ownership of who did what?" she looked pointedly between his legs. "I mean, I must've had nothing to do with any of it, even though it was me who had those babies in here for…well, not nine months, but still I carried these gorgeous little nuggets. Yes, I did," she cooed. "Oh my gawd, they are just perfect. Look at them, Kellen," Laikyn ordered.

The alpha picked up his boys again as if he couldn't help himself. "They're just like their mama," he agreed.

"Let's switch." Laikyn kissed the girls on the forehead.

"That's an excellent idea. Wait, are they smaller than these guys?" A look of horror crossed his features.

Turo left at the sound of Laikyn laughing. His need to check on Jozlyn too great. There was something about Asia and Egypt that had all his warning bells going off. They smelled like shifter, but more. He stopped to speak to Arynn, the packs omega and only other member of the Iron Wolves who could sense other beings emotions. "How's it going?" He had white blond hair and dark skin, a combination that had women falling over themselves to get to him. Add in his light blue eyes, you'd think the man was a fallen angel, yet he was one of the craziest members of the pack.

Arynn shrugged. "Not too bad. I'm glad the Fey was here; otherwise, Laikyn would have had one hell of a labor and delivery. Four fucking kids," he marveled. Who'd have thought?"

He gave a wry chuckle. "Not me, that's for sure."

"Kellen really pass out?" Arynn nudged his chin toward the room where the alpha and his mate were.

"I've no clue what the hell you're talking about," Turo lied, knowing the omega could smell the truth.

A snort was Arynn's answer. "Who's in there?"

Barely suppressing a growl, Turo had to remember he wasn't claiming Jozlyn. However, his wolf seemed to not like the idea any more than he did. "What're you doing back here?" he asked instead of answering.

"I could feel overwhelming pain and grief, but it wasn't a pack member. I thought I'd come investigate, although something kept me from stepping foot into that room." He glared at the closed door.

Not liking the idea of Arynn being pulled toward his mate, even though he hadn't claimed her, he moved, blocking the entrance. "It's nothing for you to worry about," his voice came out a deep growl, his wolf ready to emerge.

"Whoa, you need to chill." Arynn lifted his hand, touching the bunched muscles on his arm.

Turo took a deep breath, followed by another and then one more for good measure. "Sorry, I'm a little on edge. I need to go." He eased the door to the room open, not allowing Arynn a chance to see who was inside.

His gaze looked for Jozlyn, but when he only saw Asia with Egypt curled up next to her, his wolf howled inside. "Where's Jozlyn?"

Asia blinked sleepy eyes at him. "She went to get a drink." Peering at the clock on the wall, she bit her lip. "Wow, it's been over an hour since you both left. She slipped out shortly after you did."

A red haze clouded his vision. "Damn foolish human. Did she figure out we weren't one hundred percent human? Did you tell her you were something else?" What else Asia and Egypt were, was a puzzle that needed to be figured out sooner rather than later.

Asia looked down at her sleeping daughter. "I am...was a shifter. Panther shifter. Fifteen years ago, my family and I came to South Dakota on vacation. I was only seventeen myself and excited to come to America. We were going to see all the sites like Mount Rushmore and mine for gold." Her breath hitched. "While we were at Crazy Horse's park, I got separated from my parents. It was getting dark, but I figured I could find them. I mean, I'm a shifter."

Tears rolled from Asia's dark eyes, making him shift forward to give her a tissue.

"A man approached me. He was gorgeous, mesmerizing and powerful. I didn't realize until he'd taken me from the park that he'd used psychic power to subdue me. You see, my cat recognized him as our mate, but being only seventeen, I was too young in the eyes of my family. They never would've allowed me to mate so early. Especially not to this man. I don't know if I'd have found another mate, but it's a moot point now. You see, he took me, took control of my mind, and my will. For the next year, I was a virtual prisoner inside my own head. His ability is greater than any I've ever heard of outside of movies. Do you understand what I'm telling you?"

Turo didn't like what he was hearing, or what he was imagining. "Finish your story, Asia."

She ran her hand over Egypt's back. "My mate…Kenneth, that's his name, is a vampire. He knew what I was. I'm not sure if we were true mates, or if he manipulated my mind. The fact of the matter is, for the last fourteen years, since that first year, he's held me hostage with the threat of taking the one thing that means the most to me." Her gaze went to Egypt.

"You conceived his child," Turo guessed.

"My greatest blessing and most precious thing in the world. He hoped she'd be a mix of us both, but quickly realized she didn't have his traits. However, he held out hope she'd be a shifter like me, therefore an asset he could offer up to another vampire. You see, if a shifter gives their blood to a vampire regularly, then that bloodsucker can walk in the daylight without harm."

"Fuck, what a sick bastard." Turo paced the small distance from one side of the room to the other. Children were to be cherished and loved, protected from any and all harm, not bartered like a piece of furniture.

"I've acquired some of his ability since he's been drinking from me. In return, I've absorbed some of him through the bite, although he's not shared his own blood with me." She shuddered before continuing. "Through him, I've been able to dampen her abilities, making her appear more human. When he realized, or at least thought, that she wasn't going to be of any use to him, he went crazy. He beat me, demanding I get pregnant, but I was able to control my ovulation even though he was able to make me want him, which I'm sorry to say I don't know if it was his powers of persuasion or true want on my part. But no matter, I always thought of Egypt. Her safety was my number one concern. About six months ago, he took us to a cabin in the woods and separated us into different rooms. I honestly thought it was just another form of mind games until…well, long story short, I was too weak to protect Egypt. He'd drained me almost to the point of death and kept me that way for over six months, doing the same to our daughter, thinking to sell our blood to his friends, since he couldn't give them his child. With the last of my strength, I pushed a thought into one of the humans who had come to collect the latest batch of vials. He left with our blood for his employer but stopped to call about an apparent suicide attempt."

Turo was able to fill in the rest. "Where were you when they came to rescue Egypt?"

A grimace pulled at her features. "By the time they found the cabin, he'd already returned and taken me below for the evening."

He didn't need to ask for what. If he got his hands on the bastard, he would rip his head off.

"I'm sorry for what you've suffered." The words seemed hollow, but they were filled with a promise he didn't voice out loud.

"No matter what happens, promise you'll protect Egypt. My life is nothing, not anymore. I only want to make sure she never has to suffer like...please, keep her safe for me," she pleaded.

"We'll keep you both safe. I need to ask again. Is he really able to walk in the day?" The Cordell twins were hybrids whose parents were a mixture of two different species. Their father was the vampire king Damikan, while their mother Luna, was a wolf shifter. Turo knew the twins were beyond powerful thanks to their dual natures.

"Yes, but since I didn't bond with him completely, he needs to feed from me regularly." Her hand stilled on Egypt.

"Were you keeping her asleep while we talked?" Turo asked, wondering why the child never stirred.

Asia gave a brief smile. "Yes. She doesn't need to hear all the gory details of my past with her…biological sperm donor. I'd like to say there were some good times with him, but honestly, there were none." Sadness had her closing her eyes.

"You both need rest. Even with your accelerated healing abilities, you've been denied a lot, for a long time. Rest here knowing you're safe."

Bitterness turned her lips into a frown. "He won't give up looking for me or her."

Turo allowed his fingernails to shift into claws. "Let him come. The Iron Wolves will gladly show him the error of his ways. In the meantime, would you like to contact your family?"

Her breath caught in her throat. "I haven't seen or heard from them in years. I wouldn't know where to begin looking or how to contact them."

"Where are you originally from?" With her dark complexion and dark eyes, she looked Latin American, but that was a wide description. Her accent wasn't thick, but he detected the same ethnic roots.

"Originally, I'm from Costa Rica, but my mother is American, so I have dual citizenship."

He grinned at her fierceness as her chin jutted out. "Hey, I'm not planning on calling the government to deport you. Besides, we're shifters, it's not as if we belong to any one entity other than the Goddess. Now, last question before I go in search of Jozlyn," he paused. "Does your daughter have a little of both you and her bio in her?"

"Are you asking if she's going to need blood to survive?" Asia blinked slowly, assessing him like a mama bear.

"Yes, that's what I'm asking. As a member of the Iron Wolves, I need to know everything there is to know to protect everyone, which includes you and Egypt."

"Up until six months ago, she did not. Now that he has been bleeding her, I'm not sure. I suspect she will, although I don't know," she answered honestly.

"I'll find out. Don't worry, and don't let her bite you. You're already weak even if you're too stubborn to admit it." He walked toward the door, glancing over his shoulder to see mother and daughter snuggled together on the hospital bed. "I'll be back to check on you both in a few days. You can trust anyone who smells of wolf, especially Kellen Styles. He's the alpha of the pack."

Asia tilted her head in a very feline manner. "Thank you. Take care of Dr. Rasey for me. She saved my baby. Until I can repay her, I...I owe her my life."

The young woman was barely a woman when she became a mother, yet he could see she was a great mama to her daughter. "I'll do my best," he promised then walked out the door.

Lifting his head, he filtered through the scents searching for Jozlyn Rasey's unique smell. His nose twitched as he caught a faint whiff of her natural perfume. He didn't like the direction his instincts were taking him and where he was sure his little mate had run off to. "I will kill anyone who has dared to touch one hair on her gorgeous head," he growled as he picked up the pace, nearly running as he burst out the side door of the clinic after entering the code for the door to get out. He scanned the lot, making sure her car was still where she'd parked it. There, snuggled between two monster trucks her VW Beetle sat. In a few long strides, he had the door to the Iron Wolves bar open, nearly unseating Coti, who was manning the entry as bouncer.

"Whoa, hoss, slow down before you knock a human on their ass," Coti admonished.

Turo lifted his middle finger. "Where's my...where's Jozlyn, and don't give me no shit about not knowing who I'm talking about."

Coti lifted one brow. "If you're talking about that sexy doc, she's at the bar slamming shots of tequila. How a little thing like that can..."

Turo didn't wait around to hear what else his fellow wolf had to say as his eyes found his target. Jozlyn sat on a barstool with two human men on each side of her. Way too close for his liking. The one on the right gave her a high five after she slammed a shot, offering her a lime slice. Turo growled low and long as the man pulled the lime back and put it in his mouth, instead of placing the fruit in Jozlyn's hand. Before Jozlyn had the chance to accept or deny the offer, Turo grabbed him by the back of the neck.

"What the fuck?" the human asked.

"I think it's time for you to go, son." Turo gave the back of his neck another squeeze, this time making him stand on his toes.

The other man stood, coming up to Turo's chin, but had just enough alcohol to think he was ten feet tall and bullet proof. "Listen here, she's with us so go find your own chick."

Like a snake, Turo gripped him by the front of his shirt. With one asshat by the back of the neck and the other by his shirt front, Turo worked to keep his wolf in check, reminding himself they were human. "Boys, you don't want to fuck with me. I suggest you walk out that door and never come back." He lifted the man by the shirt up closer to his level, making his feet leave the floor, leaving no doubt just how outmanned he was. "Do I make myself clear?"

"We were just leaving," the one in front of him mumbled.

The man he had by the back of the neck had muttered something that sounded like 'yes, sire', which Turo took as the man was actually smart. When he released him, he stumbled, catching himself before he fell. "What the hell, man, she didn't say she had a boyfriend."

Turo nodded once, "Now you know." The muscle in the side of his jaw throbbed as he held his wolf in check.

"Wow, does that bring you lots of dates, 'cause I gotta say, it's really not working for me." Jozlyn stood next to him, her face a picture of fright.

Chapter Seven

Jozlyn watched in utter fascination as Turo tossed the two men around like ragdolls. She'd tried to ignore them, but they'd been insistent on buying her a drink. After her third tequila shot, she'd said screw it and let them buy her the fourth one. However, her fogged brain had rebelled at the thought of taking the lime from the one who'd placed it in his mouth. Hell, she was ready to lick the salt without the sour fruit, had started to pick the shaker up just as she'd felt a prickle of awareness dance down her spine. Turo. God, just saying his name made her panties wet and her nipples hard. How did the man do that to her without even touching her?

"Hello, Jozlyn," he rumbled.

Yep, just like that, her ovaries did a jig. What the hell did he do? Go to school and learn how to pitch his voice to the seduction level of panty-melting or what? Maybe she was drunk enough, traumatized enough, that it was affecting her and making her act like something she wasn't. Sure, she'd had sex. Mediocre at best with a college boyfriend. He was older, as was almost everyone she'd gone to school with. Lyric and Syn had told her having her V-card was a good thing, but they didn't understand what it was like being the only one in her sorority with it. When she'd finally done the deed, it wasn't like she'd read in books. She sure as shit didn't see stars, or feel the clenching of her vagina begging for more. Nope, Joz could only lay there hoping he'd hurry and finish.

Turo snapped his fingers in her face. "Earth to Jozlyn. Come on, I'm taking you home."

She blinked a few times, her brain fuzzy from one too many shots. "Do you know that tequila is made from blue agave and the core of the plant contains aquamiel or honey water, which is used for syrup and tequila production?"

The big, tattooed man blinked down at her, a slight grin on his too gorgeous face. "Is that right?" he asked.

"Yep. And did you know the agave plant can weigh up to two hundred pounds when harvested?" she licked her lips. Focusing on his full and very kissable mouth. She wondered what it would be like to kiss him.

"Ah, Ko'u uuku hahai, you play with fire," he mumbled.

"The Hawaiian language is so lyrical. Why do you call me your little butterfly? I'm not really that small." She slapped a hand over her mouth. "I should shut up now. When I drink, I tend to spout things. Nonsensical things."

"Like wondering what it would be like for me to kiss you?" His head bent and he brushed his lips over hers.

Words tumbled around in her fogged brain, first and foremost was the fact she clearly spoke her desire out loud. Second was the man was an expert kisser, and his lips were soft as velvet.

He chuckled against her lips. "Quit thinking and kiss me back, hahai."

Turo lifted her to the top of the bar. The others around her disappeared, or at least in her mind, they did.

"Hey, you two, get a room." Reeves smirked at them from across the bar as he cleaned a glass and set it back on the shelf.

Jozlyn was stunned to find herself with a very aroused Turo between her thighs. "What the hell are we doing?"

Turo shook his head like he'd just come out of a daze himself. "You make me lose my mind."

She smiled. "I can fix you. It's my profession." Where this playful side to her came from she had no idea, but the thought of bringing a smile to the too serious man in front of her was appealing.

He pulled her in closer to him. "You want to play doctor with me?"

Heat sizzled where they touched. "Why do I get the idea you're not talking the same kind of doctor as me?"

The naughty look he gave made her squirm in his embrace and had him inhaling. "Fuck, you smell so damn delicious. I could lick you all damn day and still want more," he growled just as the music stopped.

She looked around to see if anyone was watching them, only to gasp as several were indeed staring. "Oh my god, everyone is watching us."

Turo looked over his shoulder and growled. "Would you like to say hello to my little friend?"

Jozlyn smacked his chest. "Why are you offering me to them?"

He laughed along with the bartender he'd called Reeves.

"Should I show her your little friend, Turo?" Reeves reached below the bar, pulling out the largest gun she'd ever seen outside of television.

"What the heck is that?" Her fingers lifted to touch, but then she snatched her arm back. "Is that even legal?"

Another chuckle came from the man between her legs. "You truly are a treasure."

Her addled brain was having a hard time processing everything, which was a first for her. "I think I might be sick," she announced, placing a palm to her stomach.

Instantly the smile was replaced with concern. Turo swept her off the bar and began moving through the throng of people.

"Don't let him tap your bootyhole, girl. The wolves all like bootyhole action."

"Reeva, pipe the fuck down or I'll have your brother woop your ass," Turo snarled at the woman who yelled.

"What's she talking about?" Jozlyn rested her head on Turo's shoulder, the lurching sensation had her gulping in great big breaths of air, hoping she didn't throw up all over him.

"Ignore her," he said as he entered the ladies' room. Several women scattered as he made his way into the first stall. "Out, all of you," he ordered.

Her world spun as she was placed on her feet, but she was happy to see the toilet was clean, although her hair swung down in front of her. A second later a hand came in front of her, gathering the heavy mass and then she didn't care what or who was there as she retched into the porcelain.

"Oh god, I'm never drinking tequila again. Ever," she moaned after a few minutes.

Turo flushed a couple times so she didn't have to stare at her stomachs contents, which she was eternally grateful for.

"You probably shouldn't have drunk so much on an empty stomach. Tequila isn't bad when you do it slowly and with something to soak it up." He helped her stand. "You ready to wash your face?"

She placed both palms on either side of the stall, not daring to look behind her at the big man who'd held her hair while she tossed her cookies. Nope, never had she thrown up in front of anyone except her parents. Heck, she'd never even done it while out with Lyric and the girls. Now, this gorgeous hunk of a man not only had seen her, but he'd held her hair and flushed the yuck down the toilet a few times. Yeah, not the sexiest thing she'd ever done. "I'm fine now, you can go back…wherever you were going."

He grunted, his fingers tightened in her hair. "I was coming to find you, so I'm right where I want to be."

Chancing a look over her shoulder, she could see he was staring intently at her. "In the ladies' room with me while I said hello to the porcelain god?"

A humor filled grin split his lips. "Well, I will admit, I hadn't expected that, but you are still sexy as hell."

"You're slightly crazy. That's my official diagnosis as a doctor," she said covering her mouth with her hand. "I need to rinse my mouth out. I feel like I have swamp breath."

Turo raised a brow but stepped back, his hand still holding her hair. "Come on."

"You gonna let me go?" Her fogged brain was beginning to clear the tiniest bit.

"Do I gotta?"

His little boy lost look probably got him all kinds of things, like between any woman's thighs he wanted. The thought had her straightening to her full height, which only brought her to his chin. "Yes," she agreed.

He nodded, letting go but sifting his fingers through her hair slowly, the tips caught on a few snarls. "I love your hair. It's like black silk."

Not sure how to answer that, she went to the sink and splashed cold water on her overheated face then brought her cupped hands filled with water to her mouth, swishing the cool liquid around over and over and spit it out, repeating a couple times before she felt like her mouth was cleanish. Gah, she hated throwing up.

"Here." Turo offered her a piece of gum.

Her hands shook a little as she took the wrapped rectangular piece of minty goodness. "You're a lifesaver."

"That's what all the ladies say. Come on, let's get out of here." He held the door open.

"I need to check on Egypt." She didn't know where she was going to go. If the man chasing them was the little girl's dad, he probably knew where she lived. She'd have to check into a hotel, but if he was smart enough to get into a secured psychiatric wing of a hospital, he could probably figure out how to track her.

"Egypt is staying with her mother at the clinic. They'll be guarded by...the club members. You can rest assured nothing will be able to get to them. As for where you're going," he paused to pin her with his steady gaze. "You're coming home with me, and before you object, think. You'll be safe, since he won't think to track you there, and even if he did, I'm more than prepared to deal with anyone who dares touch what's mine."

"But, I'm nobody to you," she denied.

"You keep thinking that, hahai." He guided her through the throng of people.

Turo wasn't going to have a discussion about who she was to him at the Iron Wolves club. No, he had already figured out she was his equal. Hell, the woman was a font of information. He chuckled as he remembered her drunk rambling of useless information. Tequila facts had just been the beginning. Even while throwing up, she'd spouted information about why people vomited and how the process worked. In between her heaving, she'd pertly told him the central nervous system relayed signals to coordinate respiratory, gastrointestinal, and abdominal muscle expulsive actions. When she'd said it was divided into three stages, first nausea, retching, and then what she was doing, she'd ruined her dialogue by the next round of upchucking. However, he couldn't contain his mirth when she stopped tossing her cookies, only to continue her lesson on vomiting to tell him there was a great debate on what vomit smelled like. He'd had to tell her it smelled awful. Period! He was pretty sure his little mate had all kinds of facts tucked into her brain that would fascinate him for hundreds of years.

"I still think the studies were right." Jozlyn broke into his musings.

"What's that?"

"Well, you see, parmesan cheese and vomit both contain butyric acid, which means vomit would essentially smell the same as parmesan cheese." She stared up at him with her soulful dark eyes, and he was lost.

"Woman, you impress the hell out of me." He nodded at Reeves. "Your mind fascinates me. I can't imagine what else you know that I don't. I can't wait to find out." At the door, he stopped. "Wait here. Coti, watch her for a minute."

Before she could say a word, he stepped out of the club, needing to make sure all was secure. No way was he allowing his mate, unclaimed or not, to walk into any danger. Once he was satisfied all was clear, he went back to the door.

"That was rude." She crossed her arms over her chest.

Coti raised his arms. "I didn't say anything."

"What was rude?"

"All you have to do or say is an explanation. Don't give me orders like I'm an idiot or too stupid to understand. I'm not one of those *Too Stupid To Live* people. I actually enjoy my life and plan to stick around for the next sixty years give or take ten years or so." She poked him in the chest with each word.

His heart lurched at her estimated length of life. "I'll be sure and remember that."

Coti laughed. "Damn, I never thought I'd see the day when the big bad T was brought down by a tiny little woman."

"You want to say hello to my little friend?"

Jozlyn laughed. "I get it. Like in Scarface. Say hello to my little friend." She pretended she had a gun and began making shooting sounds.

Turo raised his head to the sky. "For fuckssake, not you too. My gun is much bigger."

"That's what he said," she laughed.

"Oh, I'll show you. Come on before I do something that'll get me arrested in most states." He joined their hands, tugging her toward her little VW.

"Whoa, big guy. I can't drive. I may have puked half my body fluids up, but I am legally over the limit." She dug her feet into the ground trying to stop him.

Turo thought of tossing her over his shoulder, but feared that would cause her to lose the rest of the contents in her stomach all over his back. Nope, not today. "I'm driving."

"Nobody drives my baby."

Hearing her possessiveness toward her little car had him stopping. "I promise to treat her like the fine piece of machinery she is. Don't worry, I know how to drive a manual if that's your issue."

She chewed on her bottom lip. "It's just…only me and my dad has ever driven it before."

"You want to ride on the back of my bike? I thought with you in your somewhat unstable condition it would be safer in your car. I could probably talk Coti out of his rig." He looked at the jacked-up Escalade sitting a little further down the lot. Coti was worse than Jozlyn when it came to his vehicle.

"Fine, you can drive, but if you grind the gears once, we get out and walk," she grumbled, handing over the keys from the purse she had strapped across her chest.

"Deal," he agreed. Hell, he'd been driving stick shifts since they'd first been invented. If he fucked up on her vehicle he should have his man-card revoked. Looking at the mint condition old Beatle, and his large form, he wasn't sure he'd actually fit inside. Man-card revoking would be the least of his worries, if he got stuck and had to call for an extraction.

"Here, take my rig," Coti said tossing him a set of keys.

Turo caught the bundle and nodded in thanks. He steered Jozlyn toward the tricked-out Escalade. "Come on, in you go." He opened the passenger door and waited until she was properly buckled in before going around to the driver's side. After a few adjustments, he eased out of the parking spot then out of the lot.

"Thank you for holding my hair back for me," Jozlyn mumbled around a yawn.

If someone would've asked him what his first night with his mate would include, he'd never have guessed anything like the one he'd had. Of course, he'd always thought he'd wind up with another shifter, not a super intelligent tiny human. "I'll always take care of you."

The drive to his place was made in silence as Jozlyn closed her eyes and slept. He watched in the rearview mirror, keeping an eye out for any suspicious vehicles. When he turned onto the exit toward his place, he turned off the lights, going in dark. With his wolf senses open, he filtered out the night sounds, searching for intruders on his property. After fifteen years, he knew each and everything that should and shouldn't be on his home turf.

Satisfied all was well, Turo pulled alongside the westside of his property, hiding Coti's vehicle from the view of the front. Jozlyn didn't stir as he got out, not even when he opened the door and lifted her into his arms. "What am I gonna do with you?" he asked, looking down into her innocent face. In slumber, she looked younger and too damn sweet for the likes of him. "I'm never letting you go," he vowed.

His back door had a retinal scanner, before the lock disengaged, thanks to Rowan Shade, their newest pack member, making it a little easier to unlock his door—for him at least. The reinforced steel swung open with a shove of his shoulder while he tried to keep from waking Joz. Again, he opened his senses, not trusting his mate's life to modern technology alone. No, he'd set his own security parameters and pull out the big guns, if needed, once he put Jozlyn to bed.

He didn't bother with any lights while navigating through the silent house, her slight frame snuggled in his arms. For the first time in hundreds of years, Turo breathed a sigh of contentment.

Kenneth misted over the SUV. The wolf inside thought he could protect her? From him? Kenneth wanted to laugh at the absurdity. Nobody was safe from him unless he allowed it. His little whore of a mate got lucky when the worthless fuck stumbled upon the cabin, while he'd been working to get his prodigy released from the hospital. He should've killed Asia before he'd left to get Egypt, but he'd wanted their child to see what happened when you crossed him. He'd planned to bring the girl back to watch as he drained the last bit of blood from Asia, but not before he'd made Egypt drink some herself. It was time his child learned what she was. Oh, yes. He'd finally figured out what Asia had been doing. Once he'd drained her enough, her mental walls had cracked enough for him to slip inside and see the years of manipulation.

A roar escaped before he could call it back, his panther DNA from his mate's blood exchange making him loose his mist form, sending him crashing to the earth. The sound of his bones snapping, pain unlike any he'd felt before had him growling, but only a slight moan bubbled forth. Lying in the middle of a tree filled forest he lay for hours, waiting for another predator to come along and think to take him out. Kenneth held completely still in the large cat's body as a deer nosed closer. He needed blood to rejuvenate broken bones and tissue. As the deer came closer, he kept his heartrate to almost nothing as his breathing was shallow. When the doe was within striking distance, Kenneth used the last of his strength to take her down, snapping the neck quickly. Usually he'd enjoy making the animal suffer, but this time, he didn't have the liberty to prolong the death. Utilizing his waning strength, he sank his fangs deep and took what he needed to begin rebuilding from the inside out. Bones began knitting and then cell by cell the regenerating process, which was excruciating this time.

The snapping and popping grating on his sensitive ears. By the time the sun was coming up, he was almost ready to move again. However, he knew he was no match for the mangy wolf, not in the shape he was in. "I will come back for you." Nobody took from him without paying. The good little doctor took his kid, and the bastard with her took his mate. How the two were connected, he didn't know and didn't care, but they would both pay with their lives.

Inhaling deeply, he shifted to mist, the form taking a lot more of his energy than he expected. No, this day Dr. Rasey was safe, but come tonight, he'd come for her and the wolf.

Chapter Eight

Jozlyn woke with a start. The first thing she noticed was her head felt like someone had hit her with a jackhammer. The second thing that came to her attention was the fact she was in a strange bed, next to a man. Of course, being in bed with a man should've frightened her, but she'd immediately recognized Turo Anoa'i from the Iron Wolves club. Her memory began filtering back to her from the night before.

"How's the head?" A deep voice rumbled next to her.

She opened her eyes again. "Um, it hurts a bit."

He nodded then got up, making the bed move only the tiniest bit. He must have one of those really expensive mattresses that doesn't disturb the other person when you move, she mused, pressing her hand down to see how far down she could press it.

"What're you doing and thinking?" he asked next to her holding a glass in one hand and a couple Tylenol in the other.

"Um, what makes you think I'm…thinking?" She sat up then squealed as she realized she was only wearing a large man's T-shirt. "Who undressed me?"

"Take these and then we'll talk." He pressed the cup into her hand, waiting until she swallowed the pills before continuing. "You didn't have anything else in your car to wear, and I'm sad to say, that although I did a great job of holding your hair, you still had a little bit of your stomach contents on the front of your jeans and some tequila had spilled on your shirt at some point. Basically, you stank to high heaven. I promise, I undressed you quickly without looking…much."

Jozlyn covered her face. "I'm pretty sure I didn't have sexy underwear on," she mumbled. *God, please tell me I didn't have old underwear on, like my favorite ones with hearts all over them.*

"You could've had granny panties on, and I'd still think you were the sexiest thing I'd ever laid eyes on," he promised.

She snorted. "Right. Pull the other one."

Turo sat next to her. "Look at me."

She kept her face hidden, embarrassment making it hard to do anything other than think of all the women he'd probably seen at their best, and here she was lying in his bed after throwing up. Yeah, she would really like the ground to open up right about now.

"I said look at me," he commanded, taking her fingers away from her face and placing them on his thighs.

Her breath froze in her throat as her fingers encountered bare skin. How the heck did she miss the fact he was wearing only a pair of boxer briefs in a sexy emerald green? "What?" she asked, licking her dry lips.

"I will never lie to you. Ever. If there's something I can't tell you, I'll tell you I can't tell you, but I won't lie."

Jozlyn tilted her head to the side. "Why?"

"Because I don't like lying, nor do I like liars. To me, it's a senseless act, and one that shows the ignorance of those who do it. If you do it once, you'll have to continue doing it, hurting all involved at some point. Yes, the truth may not always be pretty, but it's a hell of a lot better than some trumped up bullshit." He put his hand over hers. "Now, I said you were the sexiest thing I'd ever seen, and I meant it. Want me to prove it?"

Wondering how he could prove it…she gasped as he lifted her hand and placed it over his burgeoning erection. "Holy shit, how big are you?"

Turo tossed back his head and laughed. "Big enough."

"Is that what they were talking about when they said you should show me your gun?" She swallowed as his dick jerked under her palm. Her fingers automatically squeezed him, the tips unable to reach fully around his girth.

Still laughing, he halted her movements. "No. Well, not just my dick, although you could call him anything you want if you continue stroking him like that," he groaned.

Her thumb moved over the cloth covered tip. Shit, she was stroking the man's dick, and she barely knew him.

"That's not necessarily true, hahai, you know me in here." Turo touched her chest. "But, if you don't stop that now, I'm liable to make a fool of myself."

A wet spot formed where she touched him, making her wish she had the courage to pull the material back and see for herself what he tasted like. Whoa, pump the brakes girlfriend. You are not a hussy who does that sort of thing on the regular. She pulled her hand away with one final squeeze. "I need to check in with the hospital. I mean there was…" she couldn't continue when she thought of her frightened run after finding one of her co-worker's dead. "Oh god, I need to go. The police probably want to question me. I didn't even think about that. I took a patient out without permission. I," she stopped and took a deep breath. "I'm probably going to lose my license at the very least."

Turo stopped her as she tried to get up. "Easy, you need to stay calm. Jenna, you met her briefly yesterday, remember? She's taken care of all that."

Her eyes narrowed. "How did she, *take care of it?*" Jozlyn made air quotes when she said the last, making him smile.

"Trust me, please. I said I'd never lie to you and I won't. Right now, you, Asia, and Egypt need to stay off the grid. That means those two need to regenerate at the clinic, while you hide out here."

"Oh, and why do I need to be here instead of with one of my friends?"

He could see her mind working through scenario after scenario. "Because this." He lifted her chin and covered her lips with his, brushing his mouth over hers. Breathing heavily, he pulled back. "I would risk my life for yours. You don't understand what you mean to me, yet, but you will. Just put your trust in me. Give me some time, and I promise to tell you everything. I just need you to have faith."

She exhaled. "Twenty-four hours then I need to know what the heck is going on. I'm not stupid. I can handle anything if I know what it is I need to…handle."

He nodded. "How about a shower while I whip us up some breakfast?"

"That sounds good. Um, I don't have anything to wear, unless you washed my clothes last night."

Turo grinned. He'd thought about tossing her clothes into the washer, but then, she'd looked too perfect in his bed, and he couldn't resist sliding in next to her. She'd rolled into his side, slid her leg over his, and mumbled incoherently. If a bear had come charging through, Turo would've been hard pressed to do anything unless danger had presented itself to the tiny woman who'd stolen his heart. "Sadly, not yet. I'll do that while you shower. Come on, up now before you laze the day away."

Standing, he slid one arm under her legs, the other behind her back. Her yelp of surprise had him smiling. He couldn't remember the last time he'd smiled so much.

"I feel like you've carried me an awful lot in the last twelve hours or so," she muttered.

He lifted one shoulder as he set her down next to the large walk in shower. "I could carry you for days and never break a sweat. Heck, I find that thought way too appealing, hahai." Before he could make a total fool of himself, he showed her where everything was, making sure the towel was within reach for her then left her to shower on her own. He used the guest bathroom down the hall, thinking he should ease the ache between his legs then decided against it. No, the only time he wanted to release was with Jozlyn. After hundreds of years, an orgasm didn't hold the same appeal as it had when he'd been a young cub.

After drying off, he dressed in a pair of jeans and a T-shirt then padded into his kitchen on bare feet. The clock showed it was a little after nine in the morning. Figuring it wasn't too early to contact Kellen, he opened the link to the younger wolf.

"*How's the head doc?*" Kellen asked.

Turo didn't like anyone speaking about Jozlyn in a negative way. Hearing Kellen refer to her as such had his wolf growling. "*She's fucking brilliant and due respect as such.*"

"*Whoa, pump the fucking brakes. I didn't mean it in a disparaging way. Heck we could use someone like her in the pack. You are planning on making her one of the pack, yes?*" Kellen's tone suggested there was only one correct answer.

"*She knows nothing of our kind. I haven't...explained it to her yet. Hell, I didn't think I'd ever be having the talk with my mate.*" He moved around the kitchen, pulling out a pound of bacon and a dozen eggs. After checking the date on his bread, he was relieved to see it was still good.

"*Jenna would like to stop by for a visit this morning. Just so you know...it was couched as a request, but you know the Fey,*" Kellen trailed off.

"*Shit, when is she coming?*" Turo had met the tiny bundle of crazy several times and truly liked her. However, he wasn't sure if he was ready to unleash her on his unclaimed mate as of yet.

A laugh floated through the link. *"With Jenna, it could be in five minutes from the time I tell you, to whenever the hell she decides. I did tell her to be sure and knock on this link. Somehow, she's gotten a direct connection to all my pack. I swear I should just make her a member."* Affection laced his alpha's voice.

"Yoohoo, is anyone home?" Jenna asked through their link.

"Shit, woman, didn't I tell you to knock first," Kellen growled.

"If I knocked it would hurt your head, and I didn't want to wake my godchildren by popping in first. They're just so adorable. I mean have you ever seen such precious little things? I think they look sorta like me," she laughed as Kellen growled.

"Um, Jennaveve, when you planning on popping in? You know Jozlyn is completely unaware about other beings." He wanted to make

sure the woman was aware his main priority was his mate.

"Pfft, of course I'm aware. What do you think I am, a nuub? Now, I'll be there within the hour. So, if you're gonna be doing the dirty, or showing your gun off then please have it put away by the time I get there." Jenna flashed them an image of her waving and then the connection was gone.

"Jeezus, she's like a big, huge bundle of dynamite," he grumbled.

"Who?" Joz asked from behind.

Turo startled. He'd been caught up in his mental communication with Jenna and Kellen that he hadn't heard Joz enter the kitchen. Fuck, he needed to get his head out of his ass, or he could get his almost mate killed. "I was just speaking with Kellen and Jenna. She's gonna stop by here in an hour or so. She'd like to talk with you if that's alright?"

"That's okay with me. Don't you like her?" Joz moved next to him. "Can I help with anything?"

He tilted his head toward the fridge. "Jenna? She's an acquired taste, but to answer your question, yes, I love her like a sister. You want to grab the milk and orange juice? I also have a coffee maker, but it takes little pods. Help yourself."

She went to his coffee station. He stared at her backside as she shifted from foot to foot while she perused the different flavors he had in the drawer below the machine. "Oh, well that's good. Eureka," she exclaimed. "I love Breakfast Blend. Not too strong, not too weak. It's perfect."

"I'll be sure and remember that." He'd have all her likes and dislikes memorized. Now, the only problem was figuring out the minefield that was Jenna. Of course, the Fey was older than dirt and had seen most everything being created in her thousands of years of life. Surely, she could be trusted to not spill the beans on the reality of what and who he and their kind were.

"You look worried?" Jozlyn sipped from one of his mismatched mugs, looking gorgeous and rumpled in one of his T-shirts.

"I'm just wondering what Jenna is coming by for." Hell, he wasn't a hundred percent comfortable with the Fey around Jozlyn. The truth of that hit him square in the solar plexus. Kellen would probably want to kick his ass for not believing his bestie was coming for a social call, but Turo was older and wiser.

Joz offered him some coffee, but instead of having her get him one, he placed his hand over hers, holding her gaze while he took a sip of the too light brew. However, knowing she'd made the drink just the way she liked it, he wanted to experience it. The deep inhale of breath showed him she was affected by the little exchange as much as the fact his jeans were noticeably tighter thanks to his erection.

"Let's eat then we can sit on the porch and wait," he said in a husky groan. If he didn't get his mind out of the gutter, he'd likely burn the bacon. The eggs he flipped over, making sure they were over easy like she'd told him she preferred. Yep, he was totally whipped, and she'd only just come into his life.

Fifteen minutes later, Joz sat back after eating all of five slices of bacon and one egg on two pieces of toast. He demolished the rest, clearly shocking the little woman across from him. "Lord, how much can you put down, and not get fat?" Jozlyn covered her mouth. "Pretend I didn't say that."

He stood to gather the dishes. "I'm a big guy and burn off plenty of carbs on the daily." Turo couldn't tell her that shifters metabolisms were different than a human, that they burned a lot of calories when they shifted and needed more food in order to do what they did. Once he had the dishwasher loaded, with the help of Jozlyn, they went onto the back deck, which overlooked the woods. He had a nice flower garden and small waterfall with lots of plants, surrounding the entire thing.

"Oh, wow. This is gorgeous," Jozlyn said with awe in her tone.

Turo led her to the small gazebo in one corner where he thought she could get the best view. "Thank you. I like to think of nature as something you give back to. So I planted things that don't need constant watering, and when the winter comes, I take the time to pull the things out that need to be wintered and start the process over again when the time comes the following year."

"I knew you didn't just blow things up, Arturo Anoa'i. This is quite lovely," Jenna whispered as she touched one of the flowers.

They both froze as the petite woman seemed to appear out of nowhere.

"Holy shit, where did you come from?" Jozlyn asked.

"From that way?" Jenna pointed to the front of the house. Her eyes caught Turo's. "I hope I didn't interrupt anything important."

Turo kept hold of Joz when she tried to move away from him. He didn't like his mate thinking he wasn't good for anything except damage. "Oh, don't get me wrong...I love to blow shit up. Hell, I have a training course for folks who want to learn how to do just that." He loved his guns. There were a few of his things you didn't fuck with. A few of those things just happened to be guns. He saw nothing wrong with having a respect for things that went boom and could take out a mark at hundreds of feet away. Sure, he was a shifter, could kill a man or wolf with the swipe of a claw or bite of his fangs, but he'd learned through his hundreds of years and wars... human wars, that a gun could do a lot of damage and were a necessity at times. "I vet all my clients and make for damn sure nobody I train how to use one of my babies, has any nefarious deeds in mind." Jozlyn didn't know it, but they could sense lies, something she'd be learning sooner rather than later.

Jenna took a deep breath. "You realize that this one isn't going to be able to stay in the dark too much longer, don't you?"

He grit his teeth. "I'm aware. She's mine, and as such I'll handle it," he agreed.

"Why do I feel like you're talking about some major stuff here? Remember your promise, Turo." Jozlyn tried to stand, worry furrowing her brow.

Before he could say anything, Jenna held up her hand, silencing his words.

"I came by to offer some assistance of a sort. Jozlyn, your patient Egypt and her mother are distant relatives of mine. Waay distant, but their lineage is there. I've offered them sanctuary, to which they've both accepted. Well, Asia has on both of their behalf. Egypt would like to see you before they depart as one of my…err safe homes is quite a distance from here. Would you be able to come by before I pop them off this evening?"

Joz looked to Turo before answering. "Are they flying there? I don't think Asia has any ID."

Turo reached over as he saw Joz biting on her lower lip. "Jenna has, shall we say friends who can handle those things."

"Oh, like the underground thing for abused women and children," Joz exclaimed, covering her mouth as she shouted the statement. "Sorry, I shouldn't have just blurted that out. Wow, that's great though."

He could see his little mate wanted to see Egypt at least one more time before she left. Although all his protective instincts were screaming at him to keep her away, Turo knew Joz would demand she go. "Let me grab my wallet, and we'll head back to the clinic." He held his hand up as Joz opened her mouth to tell him she could go on her own he was sure. "I'm taking you, and that's the end of it. Asia's bastard of a mate is still on the loose. There's not a snowball's chance in hell I'll be letting you out of my sight for the foreseeable future, hahai."

"Awe, he already has a nickname for you. Aren't they just the sweetest things, ever?" Jenna folded her hands in front of her like she was praying. "Now, I'll just pop…err hop on out of here and see you two kids there shortly. Toodles." Jenna waved. As she was getting ready to flash away, Turo made a slashing motion with his hand behind Jozlyn's back, pointing to the side of the house.

"Don't forget to *travel* safely, Jennaveve," he growled.

"You know, I feel like a whole conversation just happened, and I was not part of it. Not to mention, she called us kiddos. She does realize we are about the same age. I mean you might be a smidge older, but I'm pretty sure she's about my age. Maybe I should do a pro bono for her. And mate, doesn't she mean husband?"

A deep belly laugh escaped Turo. He couldn't help it as he watched Jozlyn puzzling over Jenna and offering to help fix her crazy. God, he was falling for his mate. Hard and fast.

Jenna walked around the side of Turo's home smiling at the little human. She was just too cute dressed in the wolf's T-shirt, thinking she could fix her. Of course, she sort of, on purpose, called the man mate, knowing Turo would squirm, but a Fey did need to get her kicks somewhere. She wished the big wolf would've allowed her to *fix* the human and her not knowing about the shifters and others. Heck, all she'd have to do is go into her very complex mind, show her the reality of their world, and BAM. Human knows all. Jenna didn't understand why Turo was being so weird about not wanting, or rather he wanted to do the telling. "Whatever, just get to telling, silly wolfman."

"And who might you be?"

She paused at the sight of the tall shifter hybrid before her. Oh, he'd probably been a handsome man at one time. However, that time had come and gone. "My name is Jenna. What's yours?" she asked, feigning a false sense of sweet and ignorance.

He inhaled. "What are you?"

Using a bit of her power, she cloaked herself in a mantel of human. "Um, I'm a woman. Duh." She rolled her eyes and stepped into his personal space. The rot that rolled off him was nothing like the exquisite scent of her…no, she was not going to compare this oaf with the Cordell's. "Are you here to see my friends? I can take you around to see them."

An unholy light lit his features as if he'd just stumbled upon a pot of gold. "That won't be necessary. I think they'll come see me, if they ever want to see you again. A life for a life." He flashed his fangs.

It took all she had not to roll her eyes and to pretend fear she didn't feel. "What are you?"

"I'm your worst nightmare." He lunged. Using his strength, he pulled her into his body. "Don't make a sound, or I'll kill you where you stand. What vehicle did you drive here?"

Thinking on her feet, she conjured up a small compact car, one that would make him extremely uncomfortable to ride in. A Fey did have to get her kicks where she could. Waving her hand toward the stand of trees behind her, the small roller-skate on wheels sat.

"What the hell is that?"

Jenna snorted. "That's an eco-friendly car. I only have to plug it in, and it goes for hundreds of miles without leaving a footprint on the earth." Heck, she hoped what she said sounded plausible, since she was pulling the nonsense out of her ass.

He growled a curse word she was sure was anatomically impossible, but hey, she was willing to try sticking the car up his ass, for research purposes she assured her conscious. "What's your name?" She already knew it was Kenneth having coasted over his frontal lobe along with what Asia had told her, but she needed to stick with the scared human routine. Lord love a duck it was exhausting acting human and scared.

Kenneth smiled, showing off his pointy, not so white teeth. Damn, did he not hear of whitening toothpaste, she grimaced in distaste.

"My name is Master Kenneth. I would have lied to you had I feared you'd be telling anyone, but I have powers beyond those in stories of old," he boasted puffing out his chest.

Nodding, thinking he expected her to acknowledge his words, she clasped her hands in front of her chest. "What're you going to do with me?"

"If your friends value your life, they'll give me what's mine. Come, we must leave before that fool comes out."

It was on the tip of her tongue to ask him why, if he was so all powerful, he couldn't defeat the so-called fool. However, she refrained, barely.

"There's something off about you," Kenneth said as they got into her little car.

Jenna feigned a shiver. "I'm diabetic," she lied.

"Diabetic, as in you have a low blood count?" he asked with a snarl and flashing of his teeth.

"Yes, I have to have insulin, but it's not so bad now that I'm an adult and know what I can and can't eat. I mean, I'd love to be like my friends, but…oh, you don't want to hear about my childhood and how lonely it was since I had to live almost in a bubble. I mean my mama was a real germaphobe," Jenna rattled. Oh fuck, she was totally enjoying the look of horror on the idiot's face. Of course, Kellen was probably going to freak out when he finds out she allowed herself to get kidnapped, sorta, by the bad guy. Thinking of

Kellen, she sent him a mental image of her and the baddy next to her, keeping the link on their private path, knowing the vampire/shifter hybrid could have some major powers, which potentially could mean harm for her friends. An instant shout of alarm came flooding back. She knew Kellen, aka her bestie, loved her like a sister from another mister. Yep, he was so flipping his lid.

Wow, did Kellen Styles just threaten to beat her ass? She was so telling Laikyn when she saw her again. His mate really needed to keep a leash on him. Sending him an image of his mate walking him with a leash and collar while she pushed a pram holding four babies, had the alpha of the Iron Wolves yelling more obscenities. If she wasn't worried the baddy next to her would sense her use of power, she'd totally send Kellen a sense of having his mouth washed with soap.

"Um, where are you taking me? Can I call my mom?" Alright, she might be laying it on a bit thick, but geez, a girl only gets kidnapped a few times in a thousand years or so. Go big or go home, she always said.

Instead of answering, Kenneth grunted, trying to make the little vehicle go faster than the fifty or so it seemed to top out at. Jenna tapped her silver sparkly nails on her thighs and watched the trees go by, while the being next to her drove them to wherever he decided. It didn't really matter, since she was pretty confident that she could get out of any situation she landed in.

A sharp pain pierced her brain, making her squint. "Shit," she gasped.

"What?" Kenneth glared at her.

Jenna shook her head, trying to figure out what was causing the stabbing behind her right eye, hoping like hell it wasn't the hybrid next to her trying to harm her. She built up her walls, keeping them high and thick, thicker than ever before. Only those who had a link to her would be able to contact her and that was if she allowed it. She wasn't the Fey Queen for nothing, after all.

Chapter Nine

Kellen barely kept the roar of fury from escaping. His mate and children were resting comfortably, having eaten and been fussed over by everyone in the pack it seemed. Now, he had a missing Fey Queen. "God damn, Jennaveve, what the hell?" He whispered as he walked to the door, looking over his shoulder before stepping into the hall. Reeves was standing with Macon, both enforcers who were watching over his family. "I'm stepping down the hall to make a call. Nobody in or out," he instructed the two wolves.

They nodded, alert with a stillness that made them perfect for the job.

Out of earshot of the two wolves and his mate, he pulled out his cell and dialed. Sure, he could've used the mental path he'd forged with the twins, but it still gave him a bit of a…he didn't want to put words to how he felt having the wolpires in his head.

"What is it, wolfie?"

He growled, knowing instinctively it was Lucas he was talking to. "Listen up asshat. Your woman has allowed herself to be kidnapped by a being I believe was a vampire who mated a panther shifter." He let the silence hang for a second too long. "The panther born him a daughter. The child is now a preteen, who he has bled, along with the mother, almost to the point of death." He filled them in on what had transpired and waited.

"Our Hearts Love allowed a fiend of the worst sort to take her? Why?" the last was said on a roar so loud Kellen had to move the phone away from his ear.

"If I was to hazard a guess? She believes she's not in danger and did it to protect those she believes are hers. Both Asia and Egypt suffered terribly at this bastard's hands. He actually planned to take Egypt back to watch her mother die and make her drink from her. All this Jenna got from Asia's memories." Kellen turned to walk back toward his mate's room then stopped as Lucas began talking.

"Jenna is with a being who has great powers. I believe in her and her abilities. However, if this bastard takes her blood, he can also take some of her powers, therefore increasing his powers. Do you understand what I'm saying? It will be fleeting, but if he gets her vulnerable...the result could be devastating for all of us." Lucas breathed out deeply.

"Why have you and your brother not claimed her? Why? Oh, fuck, don't answer that. I know why. Jenna is stubborn through and through. Shit, what can you do? My mate just delivered our children, but I will do whatever I can."

"Felicitări, Kellen, this is Damien. For now, we'll handle the being. You take care of your mate, and...did you say children?"

"Yes, we have four. Two girls, and two boys." Pride laced his voice as he pictured his family.

"You stay with your family. Asia and Egypt, are they safe?"

Kellen thought of the way he asked the question. "Are you asking if the females are a danger to me and mine?"

"That is exactly what I am asking. If they also drank from the vampire then they will have his powers, and he can track them through their blood bond. I'm afraid they could be leading him directly to you," Damien said.

"Jenna handled the cleansing of them on this side. My worry is for her and her alone. I...nothing can happen to her. She's a part of our family."

"If I didn't know you were already happily mated, I'd have to kill you, wolfie. Now, I'll have to...I don't know man-hug you or some shit," Lucas spoke with a slight growl.

"Shit, is this the beginning of a bromance, cause I'm telling you both right now, I ain't having any part of it. Listen, we're going to begin tracking our recalcitrant love now. Before we go though, I want to impress upon you the power this being might have. He can fuck with your minds. He can take to the form of mists if he's powerful enough, or even the shape of a friend you know and trust. Rely on all your senses. If your best friend suddenly smells off, trust in your sense of smell. A vampire who's gone corrupt, meaning he's fed off his victim until they die, will smell like rot. They can mask their scent to an extent but not completely. These beings will begin to rot from the inside out. Their teeth will no longer be white, but similar to that of an addict whose teeth are decaying away. Their skin, although they can use glamour for a time, will become pale and thin. Most will begin losing their hair and will start to truly smell as if they were the walking dead, if they don't feed often. This hybrid has found a way to keep this deterioration at bay through feeding off of a shifter. He will not be satisfied with losing his food source. If he has an inkling of who or what he has in his grips," Damien trailed off.

"Find her and claim her, Cordell," Kellen ordered.

"Oh, we plan on it. Her time of running has just run out," Damien agreed.

Jenna felt Kenneth's eyes on her as she massaged her temple. "How long before we get to where you're taking me?" she asked, allowing a small bit of fear to enter her tone. To be honest, she wasn't at a hundred percent yet. Heck she hadn't been quite back to full Fey fighting form in quite a while, but she'd been a little busy finding, fixing, and all around being the best Queen of the Fey she could be.

He glared her way again. "If you don't sit there and shut it, I'll make it so you have no choice."

Her fingers itched to wipe the smirk off his face. Oh, she'd like to show him exactly who held more power, but he was her one chance to find out just how many others were like him in the region. She'd thought the Cordell men were the only hybrids. Of course, her…the wolpires were the only ones she knew of who had successfully crossed vampire and shifter genes without partaking to the last drop of a shifter. Most fangbangers couldn't resist taking the blood of a shifter. It was like the finest whisky or best drug, only the vamps didn't know when to stop, killing their blood source, which in turn made them begin to rot a lot faster than if they killed a human. Not that killing humans were any less a moral sin in her book. It just wasn't as fast a deterioration to the vampires' bodies. Human blood didn't contain magic like shifters, which also didn't increase the vampires' own powers like shifters. A fact they lusted after worse than a junkie seeking his next fix.

Jenna made the motion of her zipping her mouth, locking it with an invisible key.

Kenneth's eyes narrowed. "You're a weird human."

She lifted a shoulder. "When you're always wondering if tomorrow is your last, you learn to appreciate today for the gift it is," she said simply. She'd had so many todays that each was more than she'd ever hoped for. In all honestly, the last year or so had been the best since meeting the Iron Wolves.

They drove for what felt like hours, with Kenneth gripping the wheel tightly between his fingers, his knuckles looking bruised and as if the bones were ready to split through the thin skin. The farther away from her people, the constriction around her chest eased. He pulled into a small housing development, the homes of medium build but nicely kept.

"Home sweet home," he murmured as they drove through to the very end. The house he pulled into sat farther back from the others with woods surrounding three quarters of the lot.

"This seems...normal. You live alone?" She didn't want to search his memories out of fear he'd recognize her intrusion.

Kenneth grunted, making her think he had only a few ways of communication. Threats and the occasional grunt. A man of few words was ole Kenny, which wasn't a bad thing since she planned to end his time on earth shortly. One less baddy to breathe the precious air. In the words of a wise man, or her bestie Kellen...zero fucks would be given when he died.

"Out. Oh, don't even think of making a run for it or yelling. All the homes surrounding me are my brethren." He grinned showing off his nice yellow fangs.

Well, that answered one of her questions. She may have bitten off a little more than she could chew if she landed herself in the middle of a fangbangers party with no backup. Damn, she should have listened to the Iron Wolf. Nothing to do but fake it till you stake it, she always said, or at least she was going to after she made it out of this situation alive. Yep, it was totally going on a T-shirt.

The stabbing pain came again. Only this time, she felt the familiar brush of the Cordell's behind the pain. Knowing they were tracking her gave her a sense of relief, but worry for them came quickly on the heels of the feeling. How many fangbangers were in the nest?

"Oh for fuckssake, quit banging on my head," she mumbled, almost losing her footing as Kenneth grabbed her arm at her words.

"What are you talking about?" His fingers dug into her forearm to the point of pain.

She whimpered knowing it would be a normal reaction for a human. "I sometimes talk to myself…when I'm feeling my sugar levels drop and need to eat something." Thankfully she knew enough to spout off a little more knowledge that had Kenneth releasing his punishing grip.

"What do you need so I don't have to hear your constant whining?" The long claws on his fingers looked deadly enough any normal human would've been shaking in fear. Jenna glanced in the back of the vehicle, pointing at the backpack. "Grab it. But remember, you try anything stupid and you'll die a slow painful death. Right now, you're safe because I need you to trade for my child."

Ha, she wanted to laugh at his absurd statement. Leaning into the tiny backseat, she made sure the backpack had all the essentials a diabetic would need. Heck, she even made sure there was needles and insulin. Bam, she was totally on top of things. Every hair on the back of her neck and arms stood on end, making her acutely aware she was being surrounded by more baddies. She may need to reassess her thinking.

"Hey, guys, I see you've been trying to reach me," she said with a lightness she didn't feel, not with a half dozen vampires circling her like she was their next meal.

"What'd you bring us, Kenny?" One with a terrible comb over asked.

Kenneth's right hand flung out, his claws extended, reminding her of a weak impersonation of a horror movie villain. "She's my insurance policy in getting my brat back. All of you, get to your own homes until I call a meeting."

Another stepped forward. "You promised us shifter blood. She doesn't smell like a shifter, but I still like the way she looks."

Jenna fluffed her hair then realized he was talking about something altogether different, and she was so not on board with anything to do with the dead-men-walking dinner crowd.

"*Jennaveve, you are in so much trouble when we find you. However, we will save that conversation for later. Where are you, and who are you with?*" Damien asked.

Worried the vampires ringing her could pick up on her communication, she took a deep breath and allowed a small hole in their private path, one that would allow them to see what she did. The action would give them access to her view and private thoughts. They'd also be able to see she wasn't at her full strength and many other things she hadn't shared with anyone if they were to look. However, she didn't plan to leave them there for long, only enough time they would be able to lock onto her location. She may be brave and feel confident in her abilities, but she was not stupid.

"*We're coming to you. Stay safe, love, for if they harm one hair on that beautiful head of yours, we will do more than roll a compound,*" Lucas promised.

Turo felt a shift in the air, immediately he stood and shifted his body in front of Jozlyn. Opening his senses, he searched for what had disturbed him. Finding a lingering trace of Jennaveve with an overlaying scent of a male he didn't recognize, immediately had him calling out to Kellen.

"*Jenna's in trouble,*" he said without knocking on their mental path.

"*How do you know?*" Kellen asked, a bite in his tone.

He began moving Jozlyn into his home. He needed to get her to go back to the Iron Wolves club. No way could he leave her at his home where the intruder had clearly been. After explaining to Kellen what he sensed, he cursed as the alpha told him what the Fey had done.

"*I'm bringing Joz back to the club, where she can be surrounded by the pack. I'll go hunting for this bastard and end this now.*" He looked at the puzzled expression on his woman's face.

"I need to take you back to the Iron Wolves club. Jenna's been kidnapped by Kenneth, Egypt's father." He held her hand, felt the tremble she couldn't hide, and promised he'd kill any who was stupid enough to try to take what he claimed. Marked or not, Jozlyn was his. Fuck, he wished he had more time and a chance to explain his nature to her.

"We should call the authorities." Worry etched lines between her eyes.

Turo paused outside the hidden door to his weapons room. Taking a deep breath, he turned. "Jozlyn, the authorities can't do anything about this bastard. I promise, when I get back, everything, and I mean everything, will be explained. I would give you my heart if I could. Actually, you've had it; you just didn't know it." He took her hand and held it to his chest. "You see, when I was created, there was one woman made just for me, and that woman is you. Give me a little more faith. Trust that I would never harm you or anyone I cared for. That includes Egypt and Asia. This being who has Jenna, he has no such qualm. The authorities have no…jurisdiction when it comes to him. I'm sanctioned." He hoped like hell she didn't ask him to explain or prove as he didn't have the ability to wipe her mind or power to make her believe him. Not that he'd manipulate her in such a manner, if he could, but damn, he really needed her to trust in him.

Jozlyn nodded. "I don't know what it is, but something tells me you're…mine as well. It's weird, but when I look at you, I see every sunset and sunrise. I don't…" He covered her lips with his, kissing her like he wanted since he'd first set eyes on her. His fingers held her hips, pulling her in tight to his body.

"Goddess, you unman me, Jozlyn," he muttered between licks and kisses, his tongue following a path to her neck. The tendon where he would mark and claim her for all to see beckoned him. "Give me twenty-four hours," he pleaded.

She licked at her lips. "Okay."

The one word was enough to make his wolf back off. "I need to gather some supplies. Again, trust me when I say I'm sanctioned." They passed the laundry room, and Turo handed her a pair of shorts to put on under his T-shirt. Grabbing her hand, he led her down the hall to his safety room. He hadn't put her clothes in the washing machine as he'd said he would. Again, his mate didn't complain.

Turo placed his palms on each side of the wall, arm's length apart. The state of the art security system immediately scanned his finger and palm prints along with his unique heat signature. In seconds the wall moved back, making Jozlyn gasp. He kept his palms flat, waiting for the next level of security to pop up. He then moved his hands off the seeming normal rock walls, entering the sixteen-digit code.

"Jesus, this is like Fort Knox or something," Jozlyn marveled.

"Not quite." The final door slid back. He walked in first, making sure the room was as it should be. "I contemplated a retinal scanner but decided against it for right now."

The walls were lined with shelves holding more of his babies. He'd joked that Rowan owed him a new gun to replace the one Lyric destroyed not even a year ago. While the sweet AR-15 was a favorite, he had plenty of others. The first thing he grabbed was a large leather duffel from a storage locker. He'd need to make sure the weapons he chose, had the special bullets he'd been making, and had the appropriate bullets that would not only stop, but kill a vampire or a rogue shifter in its tracks.

Since the attack at the club where Lyric had almost been killed, he'd been working at his training facility on creating ones that would have the right projectile and efficiency they'd need. Up 'til now, he wasn't satisfied to hand them off to the women. Of course, he didn't need the same precision as they would.

"You're scaring me, Turo. What exactly are you going up against, ISIS?" Jozlyn's voice wavered.

He stopped loading the bag to turn to his woman. Goddess, why couldn't he have had just another day to spend with her before the shit storm hit? "Baby, what you see here is only a smidgen of what Asia's bastard of a mate might have in his arsenal. He's got Jenna in his clutches. I'll do whatever it takes to get that Fe...female back. No matter what happens, you need to understand you are special. If I could, I'd spend the next few years showing you exactly how special you are. I promise, when this is over, I will." He ran the back of his finger down her cheek, hoping like hell she understood.

She nodded. "There's that word again. Mate? I'm trusting you. I don't know why. Something inside me is telling me you're...safe."

Nothing could've stopped him from lifting her into his arms and taking her mouth in a kiss that seared him to his toes. He felt his teeth nick her tongue, tasted her blood, and licked it up like a man starved for his next meal. Groaning, he set her back from him. Then without thinking, he bent and licked along the seam of her lips, dipping inside at the small wound again before he moved back completely. "It's what we call someone who is a life-partner. When one of us find our one true love, we are more than married; it's our other half. I'll explain everything like I promised. You won't regret your decision, hahai."

Time was ticking, and he still needed to get her back to the Iron Wolves. Once he was satisfied he had enough fire power to take out a contingent of vampires, he sealed the duffel and led the way back out, sealing the door shut behind him.

"You would never know that room existed by looking at that wall," Jozlyn marveled.

"That's good. Come, I'll need to move quickly to get you to safety and find Jenna." Already he felt as if she was in danger and worried he would be too late.

Jozlyn held his hand as they walked to the garage connected to the back of his home. Her quietness and acceptance settled him and his wolf. When this was over, he was claiming his fated mate. Age difference be damned; she was perfect for him.

"You've gone all quiet and introspective on me. Are you scared?" Jozlyn squeezed his hand, twining her smaller fingers between his.

He looked down at their joined hands, his larger, scarred one and her perfect, unblemished one and thought again he was too hard and too old for the likes of her, but his wolf snarled a denial at him. He never went against his wolf instincts and wasn't going to start when the human part of him wanted her just as much. No, he'd just make damn sure his mate was always protected.

"No," he denied. "When I get you to the club, I'll need you to promise to not leave the safety of the pack."

"You've called them that before. What does that mean?" Jozlyn got into the truck he led her to.

Instead of answering right away, he leaned over and strapped her in, liking the fact she didn't object to his need to insure even that measure of her protection. "Twenty-four hours, hahai."

Going around the front of his rig, he checked that everything was as it should be, never taking any chances with security had kept him alive for the last three hundred plus years. His senses opened, flared wide, detected nothing amiss, he got in and opened the door to the garage.

"One day, mister," Joz said, a challenge in her dark eyes.

He nodded then backed out. The twenty-minute drive to the club was made in a comfortable, yet charged, silence. He knew when he dropped her off he'd be leaving part of himself behind.

Chapter Ten

Jozlyn knew she should be demanding answers, but something had clicked inside her the first time she'd seen the big tattooed biker. Hell, her entire body had come alive as if it had been waiting for him to arrive. Even now as he raced down the mountain at speeds that would scare her spit-less, she trusted him with her life. Her mother would probably tell her it was kismet or some other mystical thing that had drawn the two of them together. Joz, having a mind that most didn't understand would agree there was something more at play with their connection, just as she knew there was more to Turo and the people of the Iron Wolves. She'd give him twenty-four hours to do what he needed then she'd demand answers.

When the big gates to the club came into view, she was surprised to see them closed with two large men guarding them. Of course, she'd not been to the bar or club except to pick up or drop off her friends a few times, other than the other day.

However, the times she had, the gates had always been open. Fear skated down her spine as they waited for the men manning them to allow them entrance. Turo nodded at the one on the driver's side as they passed.

Turo picked up her hand. "You have nothing to be scared of here. We've shut the club down, except for members, to keep our families' safe. You're now part of that group, hahai," he said, his voice dark and full of promise.

Lord, his rich velvet tone had her clenching her thighs together. Now was not the time to get aroused, she admonished herself. "Thank you. Are Laikyn, Syn and Lyric here as well?" She didn't look at him as she unfastened her seat belt.

He inhaled deeply, shifting in his seat as if he was uncomfortable. "Laikyn and Syn are," he answered.

She swallowed as she looked at his lap, the unmistakable bulge made her wish they weren't at the club and that danger wasn't lurking around the corner. Damn Kenneth and his jackassness.

"Don't," Turo warned.

Her gaze snapped up to his, seeing the light of need reflecting back at her. "Sorry," she whispered.

His hand snaked across the distance separating them, pulling her over and into his lap. "Don't apologize for wanting me as much as I want you." He buried his face into her neck, inhaling deeply. "If I could, I'd shut us away for days and lock the world out until I sated the both of us. Fuck, you smell sweeter than the sweetest wines in Italy." His fingers gripped the hair at the back of her head, lifting her face to meet his stare. "Goddess, I need you more than I need my next breath," he swore then his lips were on hers.

Jozlyn opened for him instantly; tongues dueling. He licked at the roof of her mouth, tickling and then sweeping along hers. The action had her thinking of sex and how good he must be if his expertise at kissing was any indication. She moaned, wanting to get closer. One of his hands went to the front of her shirt, teasing her hardened nipple. It was as if the small act had a direct link to her clit, making her cry out.

Turo pulled back. "Fuck, I lose my mind around you." He glanced out the window.

She looked to see what he did, startled at the sight of two large men standing with their arms crossed a few feet from them. "Oh my gawd, they must think I'm a total hussy."

"No, they're thinking I'm a lucky, but stupid bastard. Come on, let's get you inside." Turo kept hold of her, when she tried to scramble back to her side of the truck.

Outside the truck, she stood next to Turo while he talked with the men. Her face was on fire from embarrassment. With her shoulders slightly hunched in, she didn't say a word until Turo and she walked through the door to the clinic. She expected to find Egypt and Asia, hoped to talk with them both, and see how they were doing.

"What do you mean they were moved? Where?" Anger replaced humiliation.

A blonde with rainbow colored hair held up both hands. "The alpha felt it in their best interests as well as the pack's, to move them to a more secure location. Lula escorted them herself and will return if the need arises. I'm assured she will check in regularly with updates. If you'd like to speak with her, you'll need to contact Kellen, but right now, he's dealing with his newborn quadruplets. So, your anger is a little misplaced when he's thinking about the safety of two abused females, along with the birth of his rare children which are a little more important. Basically, save the temper tantrum for someone else."

Turo moved forward to say something, but Joz held her hand up. "First off, I agree that my friends' safety is more important than any petty bullshit. Second, huge congrats to Kellen on the birth of his children. Third, don't ever accuse me of a temper tantrum unless you want to step outside, and I'll show you exactly what kind of tantrum I can throw. Feel me?" Joz was in the woman's face by the end of her last statement, uncaring if she was taller and if they made her leave for daring to do so.

"Oh, yeah. Girl fight," the man who looked eerily similar to Turo said with glee, rubbing his hands together. "I got money on the little newcomer. Sorry, Breezy, but she's got asskicker written all over her."

The woman named Breezy rolled her eyes. "I'm not fighting anyone. I also didn't mean to offend you. We're all on edge right now."

As far as apologies went, Joz assumed that was this woman's version of one. She nodded, stepping back but didn't take her eyes off of Breezy. "Just so we're clear, Egypt and Asia are not only my patients, but my friends. If anything happens to them, I'll hold everyone here responsible. And no, I won't be calling the law but kicking ass and taking names. You'll be at the top of my list." Shit, she didn't know what was making her be so aggressive, but an inner heat was boiling to a level she'd only felt one other time in her life. "And again, you all have strange words for each other, which I'm sure is another thing you're going to explain." Joz stared at Turo.

Turo nodded, his reassuring presence had her calming. "Hahai, I promise you that both Egypt and Asia are safe. Safer than anyone in the world right now."

She glanced over her shoulder, taking in his honest look. "Fine. Twenty-four hours. What am I supposed to do until then? I thought I'd be here helping my…friends." She bit her lip not wanting to show weakness in front of the others. She didn't mind Turo seeing everything about her but not the others.

"You're a doctor right," Breezy asked.

Joz looked back at the other girl. "Yes," she agreed.

"We're preparing for what might be emergencies. Our men are going out to…see about taking care of threats against us. If a worst-case scenario happens, we could use all hands-on deck, especially with Laikyn out of commission. I know you're a…head doc and all, but I'm assuming you know something to do with medical issues?"

Joz wanted to laugh. She had a lot of spare time on her hands and had probably read more than most surgical doctors. While she may not have as much practical time, she'd also done clinicals for fun. Yeah, she was a total nerd and fine with it. "I think I can help out some," she said without going into detail.

Turo looked at the clock and then turned Joz into his arms. "I need to make tracks. You stay inside. Don't go out unless you have Coti with you." He nodded at the man who resembled him.

Coti smiled, showing off his stunning grin. "I'll stick to her like white on rice."

Turo growled. "Not that close, fucker."

"Hey, I take this whole guard duty very seriously. She's gotta go potty, I'm there. She's gotta go…" Turo made to move toward him, making Coti laugh and put Breezy in front of him. "Just kidding. I know she's your mate, man. Go, she's as safe as a nun in a convent with me." He winked.

"Goddess save me from asshats. Coti, one mark on her beautiful body and I'll skin you alive," Turo warned then left without another word.

Joz placed her hand over her heart, wondering why he hadn't kissed her again. Of course, she realized when they tended to get close, the world disappeared.

"All of our men tend to get all growly and protective. Come on, I'll show you where we've began setting up just in case," Breezy said.

"Um, do you have some extra scrubs I can borrow. I didn't think I'd be in need, you know." Joz indicated her attire. Her face felt on fire as she looked down at the men's T-shirt, and basketball shorts she wore.

Breezy laughed. "Of course. You're about Laikyn's size. Well, her size before she got knocked up with four babies. Can you believe it? Hell, I'm freaked over the idea of one, let alone four."

Jozlyn couldn't believe her old friend Laikyn had four babies either. She'd just come to grips with Lyric having a child unbeknownst to her. Now, her other friend had gone and delivered quads. Yeah, her world was totally being knocked off its axis. Next thing she'd find out, Syn was gonna be having a few, and she'd hear there really were aliens at area fifty-one or some off the wall shit.

As Breezy got her a set of scrubs then began showing her around the clinic as they called it, she was impressed with the level of medical care they could offer.

"What, did you think this was some hillbilly operation?" Breezy pushed the door to the breakroom open. "Before you get your claws out, I'm not being bitchy. I actually think you and I will be great friends. Of course, your mate needs to get to the explaining so there's no barrier between us."

Joz wondered at the last bit. What could possibly be between them, other than a little attitude in the beginning? She opened her mouth to ask then closed it as Breezy pulled her phone out of her pocket, her eyes lighting up. Joz was sure it was a trick of the lighting, but for a moment, she thought her new colleague's eyes had changed.

"That was Xan. He wanted to let me know they were almost to extraction point and all was looking good." Breezy held the phone to her chest, taking a deep breath.

"Are you okay?" Joz put her hand on the other woman's arm, her tension unnerving.

Breezy raised her head. "Oh, yeah, he's a little intense sometimes. You know how alphas can be." She turned away.

Joz had heard the term being bandied about more than once, filing it away in her mind until she and Turo had their talk. The man definitely had some explaining to do.

"Is Laikyn up for visitors?" She hadn't wanted to seem too excited until now, but the need to check on her friend and the four infants had her asking. In the tour of the clinic, Breezy hadn't shown her where any of the current patients were. Of course, she didn't understand why they would have patients instead of them going to the hospital. Heck, with Laikyn having four babies, surely preemies, they should have been delivered at a hospital that specialized in those types of births.

"Oh for sure. Come on, I bet she's dying for company right about now." Breezy's longer stride led the way down a hallway. They came to a set of double doors with Coti trailing behind. "Coti, you realize you're going to be blessed with the vision of the next generation of Styles, right?" Breezy's fingers flew over the keypad.

Joz's mind filed the combination away automatically. Had nobody told Breezy of her ability? Oh well, it wasn't her fault, and it wasn't as if she was going to give access to the clearly private wing to anyone.

Coti snorted. "Ah hell no, I'm not. I don't want anything to do with the little cubs, err, babies until they are big enough to walk on their own. Nope, I'll just sit right outside the door until y'all are ready to roll out."

Breezy coughed a word that sounded like pussy, but she smiled and kept on walking with her fast stride. Joz knew exactly which room had to be her friend's as the blue and pink balloon arch clearly proclaimed it as such.

Nerves and a bit of excitement had her placing a hand over her stomach. The other woman gave a slight tap on the door before she pushed it open. Joz assumed it was okay to follow. Her eyes took in the sight of three little babies in cribs. She'd expected to see isoletts, or incubators since most who have multiples tend to need them. However, Laikyn was sitting up nursing what looked like an average sized new born.

"Joz, I'm so happy to see you. Um, are you on rotation?" Laikyn looked to Breezy then back to Jozlyn.

She shook her head, walking over to look at the other babies. Each one had a healthy glow. "Wow, they are gorgeous." Intelligent blue eyes stared back at her from the two little ones who had to be boys with their blue sleepers. Looking to the next crib, the little girl slept peacefully. She too looked as if she weighed at least seven to eight pounds. "Laikyn, how much did each of these little ones' weigh?" The resemblance was clear who their father was, but damn, if her friend had four children this size in her just yesterday, she had to have been as big as a house.

"The girls each weighed in at just over seven pounds two ounces. The boys of course were over achievers, weighing seven pounds eight ounces each. Identical in every way." Pride laced her voice.

The little girl began to squirm in the small crib, a slight mewl puckering her lips before she gave a little cry. "May I hold her?" Joz asked.

"Of course, but I must warn you, she's gonna be ready to feed. It's her turn." Laikyn removed the little one she'd been feeding from her breast, placing her on her chest, patting the child while she watched Jozlyn.

"Oh, my goodness, she's gorgeous." Joz looked at the utter perfection of the baby. Something had her gaze going back to the two little boys, startled to see them staring at her as if they were ready to attack. She laughed at the silly thought.

"I know right," Laikyn agreed.

Joz met her friends' bright blue eyes. "Congratulations. I mean, wow. Two identical twin boys, and girls. That's like really rare. There are only," she stopped as Laikyn stared at her.

Laikyn kissed the little girl she held on the cheek. "Don't even start with your numbers, woman." She laughed, taking the sting out of her words. "I can only hope my babies are half as smart as you. Breezy, did you know she's like the smartest chick ever? Don't shake your head at me, Jozlyn Rasey. She has that memory…you know, like that guy from Big Bang Theory, Sheldon. Yes, she does. Oh yes, she does," she cooed down at the baby. "Syn and Lyric would always talk about you, saying I was almost as smart as you. I confess, I was a little envious when I was going through med school."

"It was a bit of a…hindrance growing up. Most people looked at me weird except Lyric and Syn and then you. Now, you've done something amazing." Joz indicated the babies.

Breezy raised her brows. "You're both pretty awesome."

The baby in her arms began to fuss. "Switch?" Joz asked. "By the way, how do you tell them apart?"

Laikyn pointed at their wrists. Each child had a little gold bracelet with their names engraved on them. Passing Everleigh over to her mama, she took Enzley into her arms. "That's pretty clever, but what happens when they start moving around?"

"Oh, Jenna said she'd help with that." Laikyn had Everleigh nursing while Breezy held the two boys now.

"You realize I feel as if I'm in the Twilight Zone, right?" Joz took a deep breath and waited. She'd heard several of the ladies had memories similar to her.

Breezy got up to put the two boys back as Syn knocked on the door. "I need to make a call. You guys stay here, okay. Coti is outside and Laikyn, you know what to do if you need anything."

Syn went over to the bed and glanced down at the babies laying there. "Can I hold one?"

"Of course. They're your family and besides, I'm gonna need all the help I can get with these four little angels, especially when they..." She and Syn exchanged glances.

Joz tilted her head to the side. "I really wish I could ask you to be truthful to me without messing with my promise to Turo."

"I knew it," Syn exclaimed, jarring the little one she held. "Sorry, sweetie. I knew you two were mates. This is wonderful. Now, we just need to get NeNe a wo...man here."

Was her friend getting ready to say woman? Cause she could just pump them brakes on that one. NeNe was crazy as all get out, but she was in her own words *all about the dick*.

Turo, Reeves, and a few other pack members rolled up to the quiet cul-de-sac. The scent of vampires filled his lungs. "He's here." Sending back the info to Kellen, he wasn't surprised to get an immediate reply that the Cordell's were enroute, if not already on site. "We'll have some back-up in the shape of the wolpires, boys."

He hated the time it had taken to get to the location. Each mile away from Jozlyn ripped at his soul.

Xan's XV came to a stop next to him. His passenger window rolled down. "Sun's up. You think they're still sleeping or what?"

Turo noticed the other wolf was glaring out over the steering wheel as if he could see through the walls of the houses. "Without the Fey here, or the Cordell's, we're gonna have to do this the old-fashioned way."

Xan's lips kicked up in a grin. "I really do like it when you talk dirty, Turo. Did you bring your big gun with you?"

Nate, one of the younger wolves lifted the straps to his duffel up. "Pretty sure he brought more than just one."

"Me and these guys are gonna go in on four legs. You and your crew go in on two. Keep your senses open, but remember these are vampires we're dealing with. Damien and Lucas said they can fuck with our minds if we let them. The only link I want open is the alpha path. Kellen is linking all of us. If someone is in trouble call out through that path and that one alone. Keep your walls up high and tight. Got me?" Xan looked at each man, his blue laser stare showing all he was acting alpha and head of the mission.

Turo nodded. He wasn't going to get into a pissing contest with Xan or any of the other wolves. They were there to get the job done. Kill the beings who dared to hurt his mate and innocents alike. "What're you gonna do with your rig?" he asked jerking his thumb at the unmistakable vehicle Xan drove.

With a wink, the other wolf began reversing quickly. Turo's phone rang, Xan's number showing up on the caller ID. "What's up?"

"There's a park a block back. It was empty and looked somewhat safe. I mean, at this point, I figure we're going into a shit show. You want to follow me and we'll shift there or are you just gonna roll up with your guns blazing?" Turo lost sight of Xan as he turned a corner.

"I'm driving in. Something tells me I'm gonna need my rig to move fast." He never ignored his instincts, and they were screaming at him.

Silence distended through the line. "You can move fast on four legs, T. What's going on?"

Xan's question had him rolling his shoulders. He didn't know what had him driving through the quiet neighborhood with all his feelers open. For all he knew, Jenna was holding the vampires' hostage. However, his gut told a different story. "Shift and stay safe, Xan." Breezy would flip her lid if her mate were hurt. An image of Jozlyn popped into his mind. He would move heaven and earth to have what Xan and Kellen had.

"You worry about your own hairy ass. I got my shit covered." Xan disconnected as the sound of his vehicle quieted.

Turo and the wolves in his truck didn't say another word as he drove, their focus on each house as they passed. When he got to the end, the larger home, which sat a little further back, had a glow only someone who'd been Goddess touched would notice. "Looks like we've found our Fey and more than likely, a vampire who's sampled from a panther shifter. He's gone without his fix for a while now. However, that only makes him even more dangerous."

Reeves grunted as if in agreement.

Turo knew the vampires would have felt their arrival. He was banking on the fact they hadn't risen as the sun wasn't due to set for another hour. Of course, being the fucker had basically drained Asia and Egypt, he could very well be sitting inside with a full contingent of his brethren waiting to fall upon

Turo and his pack. Well, they'd have a fight on their hands. "Reeves, you and Macon grab your choice of gun. If at any point you need to shift, drop the gun and do it. Don't worry about my babies. They're replaceable."

"Holy fuck, did you really just say that. Mac, I need you to be my witness that Turo's done lost his damn mind." He pulled out an automatic weapon, grabbing a box of bullets and loading quickly.

Shaking his head, he held his hand out and waited for Macon, aka Mac to give him his favorite gun. His friends can laugh and joke all they wanted, but when it came down to it, their lives were worth more than some metal and lead. Or in this case, their bullets were made up of silver that had been specially made with the help of the Cordell brothers. They could stop and kill a vampire and shifter.

"Reeva told me to explain to you in no uncertain terms that I was not to come to any harm as she feels it too," Reeves stepped out of the truck, slamming the door as he said the last word.

"I'll do my best to keep your pansy ass safe…for Reeva's sake. However, I have it on good authority that she has built her walls up to keep you from feeling her shit, so I'm pretty sure you can do it too, pussy." Turo punched him in the arm.

"See, she's probably wailing in pain right now." Reeves laughed as they all met in front of the truck.

Macon shook his head. "You know, we sort of look like a ragtag bunch of gun fighters, only cooler."

Tipping his head back, Turo sighed. "Let's go, pups. Remember, only shoot to kill. We ain't taking prisoners here."

"Yes, sir," Reeves said clicking his shitkickers together.

"Fucker," Turo growled.

A swell of power washed over them, making Turo raise his gun toward the land off to the left of the property, making the woods now look ominous. Shit, his pack mates were coming in from one of the surrounding areas. "I don't like the feel of that." He held his hand up.

Macon walked up to his left, with Reeves on his right. "Do we go into the house or check out what's out there?"

"It could be a trick the vampires use to keep people from coming into the homes while they're at their most vulnerable. Xan and the others can protect themselves. Let's go. If they need our help, they'll call out." As a unit, they moved forward. His wolf pushed to the front, taking in every scent. Jenna's stamp was everywhere, even though she'd clearly been trying to cover it up. Although he sensed human overlaying her, he recognized the Fey.

"Jenna is here," he told them on their private link. *"From what I can tell, her Fey blood has been spilt."*

"Good, get in and get out. Kill every fucker who gets in your way," Kellen growled.

Turo looked at the door. The nondescript entrance didn't appear to have any type of security attached to it, other than the ominous warning still pulsating from the woods. *"Weapons ready and it's a go."* Turo tried the knob, finding it locked. Using his shoulder and his wolf's strength, he shoved hard, breaking open the door. As they entered, scents of blood and sweat assailed them, along with rotting flesh.

"Fucking-A, man. What the hell are they doing here?" Mac asked with his fingers pinching his nose.

It took a moment for Turo's eyes to adjust to the darkened interior. The vampires had clearly not cared what their homes looked like to outsiders. He wondered if poor little Egypt had been forced to live in such filth, but he didn't catch even a hint of her scent. The open floor plan allowed him to see into the kitchen, which was covered in what appeared to be trash and rotting human corpses. The vampires had two of them on the table as if they were a buffet to be shared. "It looks as if they had a party and forgot to clean up." Disgusted with what he was seeing, he moved through the mess, focusing on Jenna. The Fey was there. Goddess, he hoped Jenna hadn't seen what they were...Fey or not, a female didn't need to be witness to the depravity they were seeing.

Chapter Eleven

Jenna sensed the shifters above her. When Kenneth had left her with the group of vampires, she wanted to follow, but then they'd brought in the woman and child. Goddess, a vampire woman and child, starved for nourishment. It was all she could do not to offer her own blood to the too thin females. Mother and child hovered in a corner while the half a dozen cowardly men kept taunting them. She'd seen the blood bags they'd tossed around, just out of reach of the females. If she wasn't supposed to be helpless, she'd have flashed across the room and given them a taste of their own medicine. However, the stench from upstairs kept her from ghosting up to route for more of the precious blood. Gah, these bastards needed to die a slow death.

Red eyes turned to her. "Kenneth isn't here any longer. What'd you say we have a little taste of his latest pet?"

Having so many spawns of hell focused solely on her, she truly did wonder if she might have bitten off a bit more than she should have. Her own powers were at an all-time low after healing Asia and Egypt plus helping deliver four babies, not to mention she had yet to recover fully from...no, she wouldn't allow herself to think she couldn't handle these fiends. The shackles around her wrists and ankles were heavy, would definitely hinder a human. Jenna would only have to imagine being free and she would be. "You really don't want to do that. I ate a fuckton of garlic just yesterday. I can actually taste it still on my own tongue," she lied.

One of the bastards laughed. "Oh, that is rich. She'd believes the tales like all the other stupid humans. Well, there's no time like the present to school you on your ignorance." The speaker stepped forward.

"Goodness, you really should see someone about that...I mean all of you need to see a doctor. Acne is treatable. Maybe decaying skin is as well. I know a really good doctor who might be willing to help you." She had a moment to enjoy their stunned looks before their fangs flashed down. "Yikes, what big ugly teeth you have, too. Didn't your mothers teach you the benefits of brushing?"

"Bitch, you are so gonna die a slow painful death by my teeth ripping out your throat," a vampire hissed.

"Louis, she's trying to get a rise out of you. Calm yourselves at once." A vampire spoke from a darkened corner.

Jenna stiffened. She hadn't sensed his presence, which worried her. "From the looks of you all, I don't think there's much to rise, except maybe the stink levels." She waved her hand in front of her face.

"Ah, you are a funny one, human," he said, his words almost lyrical.

She barely resisted the urge to flash from the basement, but this being was what had made her allow Kenneth to pseudo kidnap her. Yes, she could tell he was much more than just a low-level vamp like the six beings backing away in fear. Their mutters of Master also sealed the deal on her assumption.

"I'm just trying to keep my sanity in a world that seems to have gone a little cray, cray, you know?" she asked, watching as he moved toward her. His movements reminded her of Damien and Lucas. A mantel of control and seduction in their every move. Only this being did nothing for her as a woman, except make her want to hide. Heck, she hadn't been afraid of anything or anyone in a millennium or more.

He inhaled deeply. "No, it's more than that. You are more than you are pretending to be, but I can't quite put my finger on it. Maybe…I should sink my teeth in a little further and then all your secrets will be told," he said, flashing to her side.

Jenna was too stunned by his assertion she hadn't been aware of his movements, or prepared for his sudden appearance in front of her. Her gasp was born of fear and shock. "Kenneth will not be pleased."

The vampire laughed. "You think I care about Kenneth or what pleases him? He is not the Master

Vampire he thinks he is." His head bent, tongue flicking out and licking at her neck.

She felt frozen in place then she sensed them. Her wolves.

"Ah, intruders, I fear. Never worry, I shall dispatch with them in due course and return to you shortly. While I'm gone, don't go anywhere, my lovely." He trailed an elongated nail across her cheek, making it sting. Blood. The scent of her blood hit her and the demon in front of her. His black eyes flashed to red. The other vampires flew at her, but the being who'd cut her put his body in front of hers.

Her cheek felt on fire, poison filling her veins from the cut. "Damien…Lucas," she murmured.

The vampire's head turned toward her, red eyes watching her with intent. "Oh, this is going to be so fun."

Her vision wavered then darkness took her.

Turo kicked the door to the basement open as soon as Jenna's scent became all Fey. Her blood had been spilled. His wolf clawed for supremacy, wanting to rip the throats out of any who'd dared touch the tiny female. His boots pounded down the steps. Not bothering with the final level, he launched himself over the railing. Landing on his feet, he stood and came face-to-face with half a dozen or so vampires in the middle of bloodlust.

"Say hello to my little friend," he growled, unloading the weapon on the first two who charged at him. The looks of horror on their faces as they felt the impact of the first few bullets brought a smile to his face. He sprayed the next one with several more bullets, his gun hitting true as he killed another one.

Macon and Reeves came up behind him, their guns up and ready. "T, this is a tight place to be spraying bullets. Where's J?"

His gaze went to the tiny woman on the ground, the shackles on her wrists and arms looking too big for her small form. "Go get her, I'll take out these fuckers."

The remaining three vampires were snapping their teeth at him like rabid dogs. Turo lifted his weapon and fired into one of them until he had no more bullets, a grin on his lips the entire time. His hand went to his back, grabbing the spare gun when he was shoved in the side. He glanced down to see a child, a young girl who couldn't be older than ten hitting him with both fists. Her red eyes told him she too was a vampire. "Fuck, we got a kid vamp." He held his gun up and out of her way as the last vampire tried to go for his throat. No way was he letting go of his gun or the kid. Using the AR-15 like a bat, he knocked the vampire upside the head. While the being was stunned, he raised the gun and aimed again.

"No, he's my father," the child cried.

"God dammit, he's going to kill me. Hell, he's killed many. Look at him," Turo roared. The man's skin was barely hanging onto his body.

A woman with red eyes crawled over to where the little girl was hanging onto Turo's arm. The vampire, seeing a shot to escape, headed for the stairs.

"Don't let him go. He'll only hunt you down or worse, those you love," the woman whispered.

Turo felt for the woman and child, but no way in hell was the bastard getting out alive. However, he did have compassion for the females. "Cover her eyes," he ordered then he launched himself up the stairs, grabbing the vampire before he could make it to the top, snapping his head with his bare hands. The long knife strapped to his thigh was the only weapon he had on him that would be soundless. Using the sharp blade, Turo sliced through skin and tissue, severing the man's head. He took it and the remains up top, hiding him from view of his family as best he could.

A feeling of being watched had him looking through the darkness. He shook his hands out and waited for whatever was there to come at him.

Moments later, the back door flew open then the Cordell's came through on a gust of wind.

"Where is she? We can't feel her anymore?"

Turo wasn't sure which was which, so he pointed down, unsure if they were the presence he was feeling. Kenneth hadn't been in the basement, nor could he sense him. *"Kellen, how's our women?"*

"I'm with Laikyn right now. Jozlyn is sitting with Breezy reading a magazine. All is well here. Did you find Jenna?"

He explained the Cordell's had shown up and that he was about to check on things when a bad feeling had hit him. Kellen reassured him Jozlyn was fine. Ending the link with Kellen, he went back down to the basement. His eyes found the two female vamps huddled together in a corner, while Damien and Lucas knelt next to Jenna.

"What the fuck happened here?"

"Tone, boy," Turo said as he came to stand by them.

"I've not been a boy in over three thousand years, pup. You may be older than the rest of them wolves, but you're nothing compared to me and Lucas. Now, I asked a question. What. The. Fuck. Happened?"

Turo didn't give two fucks how old or angry Damien and Lucas were, he wasn't a whipping boy for anyone, least of all vampire/shifter hybrids. Pulling the gun he'd had hidden from his back, with enough firepower in it to kill the man in front of him, Turo placed the barrel under Damien's jaw. "You may be old as shit, have powers to rival my Fey Queen, but you don't talk down to me. Now, I'm gonna answer you 'cause I feel like it...," he pulled a second gun faster than the eye could track and had it trained on Lucas. "I'd hate like hell to hurt Jenna's mates, but seriously, you both are pissing me the fuck off. Like I was trying to say, I've no fucking clue what happened. When we came down, there were six fangbangers and two female vamps. Jenna's scent was cloaked as a human, until moments before we entered the basement."

He looked down to see the normally perfect complexion of the Fey Queen was a sickly green. Her veins were completely visible, as if she had transparent skin.

Both the Cordell's took a step back and were kneeling next to a slow breathing Jenna. The one he thought was Lucas looked to the vampire female. "What did you see?"

The female shook her head.

"You better answer now, or I'll kill you and your offspring." Cold hard resolve hardened his voice.

"A vampire who can walk in the day came here yesterday. He looked right through us like we were nothing, but when Kenneth tried to take Malia from me because he wanted to punish me for not drinking from a human, the stranger stepped in. He floated over to the woman then when he was getting ready to bite her, they came." She pointed at Turo. "He cut her cheek, said something about fun, and disappeared. I've never seen that before."

"Lucas, if this vampire can walk in the day, he could be like us. But, why would his cut poison our mate?" Damien looked at the small slice and bent to lick it, stopping as his brother pulled him up short.

"We don't know what it could do to us. We need father."

No sooner had Lucas said the words, when the entire house rattled like a tornado was about to shake it off its foundation. The two females hugged each other.

"Where is she?" Damikan asked, appearing out of thin air.

Damien and Lucas both held her hands, as their father examined the Fey Queen. Turo watched, wondering why they couldn't give her their blood and fix her.

"She is in grave danger. I must take her back to the castle. You two will come with me. There is much you don't know that needs to be discussed." His dark gaze turned and pinned the two females with his stare. "You will come as well as I can sense a great hunger in you. We will make sure you are taken care of and given the best care."

The woman began to cry, her child sensing her mother's fear put herself in front of her mother. "You can't hurt my mommy. I won't let you."

Damikan moved in front of the child with ease, lowering himself to one knee. "Nay, I will not and nobody else will in my home either. You are going to be a fierce warrior, when you grow up. Come, time is of the essence." He touched the matted hair of the little girl, cleansing her of the filth and grime. Her mother gasped and touched her daughter's blonde hair. Damikan did the same to her. "Now we must go." He swung away and motioned for them to follow.

"Who are you?" the little girl asked.

"He's your king, little one," Turo answered.

The woman's eyes misted over, red tears fell. "We are not worthy."

Damikan turned back around. "I have searched you and your child's mind. You are worthy. Don't say such negativity against yourselves again. Now, my future daughter-in-law is in peril. Come," he ordered.

Several men materialized beside him. "Take the two women to our healer and have them looked after. Make sure everyone knows they are under my protection."

One of his elite guards bowed then touched both women, and then, they were gone.

"Fuck, I really need to know how you do that disappearing shit. It sure would've made getting here a lot quicker."

The vampire king lifted one brow. "Oh, trust me, it's a lot more taxing than you imagine. That soldier will be down for days. He'll sacrifice some comfort for what he's done."

"You all just appeared without any apparent issue." Turo waved toward Damikan and the three men standing guard.

"Ah, well, I'm a little different. I brought them with me. Sending him back with the two women, he had to do on his own. Listen, you want a lesson on my kind?" Damikan bent and picked up Jenna. "I'm gonna need you two to release your hold on her." He pinned Turo with his black stare. "When you want a full lesson, give me a call. I'll be glad to fill you in. I have a feeling you thirst for knowledge."

He nodded then watched as the contingent of vampires and the Cordell's disappeared. A moment later all the blood and gore in the home were gone too. "Well, that certainly made the cleanup a lot easier. Anyone heard from Xan and the others?" Reeves asked.

They headed back up the stairs, happy to see even the upper floors were cleaned of the stench of vampires. "I must say them boys sure do know how to take care of business," Macon said.

Turo growled. "Hey, I think we had shit under control." He lifted his gun to make his point.

"Oh, right. Plus, you get major cred for threatening the life of Jenna's mates."

"What the fuck, T. I leave you unsupervised for all of fifteen minutes and you tried to start a war?"

Xan asked as he strolled in wearing a pair of jeans. He looked like he'd just shifted.

"Did you see any vamps?" Turo ignored the aggression rolling off of Xan.

The second to Kellen shook his head. "We went through every house here. They were lived in, but no sign of any beings there." Xan took a deep inhale. "Now, about this potential war?"

"You're like a dog with a bone," Turo groaned then explained what had happened in the basement.

Xan's posture straightened. "So, your guy wasn't here?"

The fact Asia's old man was nowhere to be found bothered him. He glanced around the interior of the home, looking for anything that would give them a clue as to where the man might've gone. The only one who could've told them anything was too sick and possibly on her way to being mated to the wolpires. Shit, an urgency to get back to his own unclaimed mate had him moving toward the door.

"Let's get back to the club. The fucker's like a god damn tick." Turo raised his head and opened his senses. He hated not being able to trace the being.

"Alright, I'll bite. What are the parallels between the two, other than they both like to bite?" Xan asked walking down the sidewalk next to him. He motioned for the rest to climb into the back of Turo's truck. "I've got shotgun until we get back to my rig, puppies."

Turo sighed as he got in. "You know a tick likes to leech onto a being and suck and suck until they're big and fat, and they're ugly motherfuckers. Well, Asia's old man is even worse than that. I'm gonna enjoy popping the fucker's head off and watching him bleed out," Turo promised.

"You realize you just made me throw up in my mouth a little, right?" Xan placed one arm on the door with the window down. "Let's roll out, T, my mate is in need of some baby making practice."

Rolling his eyes, Turo headed toward the park where Xan had left his XV.

Kenneth glared down at the shifters as they left one of his homes. He couldn't sense any of his men inside, the total emptiness reeked of a master. One that made Kenneth seethe in anger. "Who dared to come into my lair and take what's mine?" He looked at the vampires he'd taken with him, the four newly made vamps hadn't yet begun to rot like the six he'd left, making it easier for them to blend into society. They also brought with them a fresh influx of cash, which helped keep them in the lifestyles they were accustomed to, without having to wipe the brains of humans. Not that Kenneth couldn't take what he needed when he required it. However, having new blood was what a lair needed. He reached out to his other soldiers, the ones he'd sent to watch over the Iron Wolves club. Oh, he knew they thought they were safe locked behind their reinforced steel, but he had ways of getting around such things. He looked at the young vamp next to him. Oh yes, the young man was an easy mark as he'd left the club two days ago.

Humans want power and wealth. Greed made for easy manipulation if you had abilities such as Kenneth. He'd followed the young man home, taken over his mind, and now, he'd have an entrance to the club. It's as easy as taking candy from a baby. He'd show the inferior wolves how much of a tick he was as he sucked the life right out of their mates. Luckily, he still had vials of Asia and Egypt's blood, giving him a boost to his powers. For now, he'd need to find out what happened to the rest of his people then he'd get his family back and make them all pay for interfering in matters that didn't involve them. Hell, if it wasn't for the little doctor and her nosiness, he'd have taken Egypt from the hospital and never known about the other shifters. "Well, it doesn't matter now. I know, and now, my brethren, we can all have the shifters' blood feeding us."

Once he was sure the shifters in question weren't coming back, he went into his home. The clean, almost spotless place startled him. This was the work of a magician or something he didn't want to think about. If a master vampire strong enough to wipe out his entire nest and take something he'd claimed without leaving a trace…no, Kenneth wouldn't contemplate that there was a being higher up on the food chain than he. He had shifter blood running through his veins. He could tolerate the sunlight for short periods of time and shift into mist and other beings. He was the master around here. Inhaling deeply, he realized there was nothing for him to sense other than the wolves, and their smells were offensive to him. "The only thing those beasts are good for are feeding from," he growled.

The men around him stepped back, giving him a feeling of superiority. Oh, they understood who was the one in charge. Yes, it was going to be fun teaching the worthless dogs the same when he took what was most precious to them. "You take my mate and child, I'll take yours," he promised darkly.

Chapter Twelve

Jozlyn put the magazine down and picked up another medical journal. This one was on the latest development for experimental research in cancer patients. A half hour later, she laid it next to the stack of other things she'd read.

"Have you not found anything you want to read?" Breezy asked waving at the stack of items.

"Oh, they're all interesting." Jozlyn looked at what the other girl was reading, seeing a book on wedding dresses, Jozlyn's eyes lit up. "Are you getting married?"

Breezy waved her left hand back and forth. "Yes. I mean we're already mates, but…I mean it's…well, back to you. Why haven't you settled on one of those." Breezy pointed at the stack of books.

"I read them all," Jozlyn said with confusion lacing her voice.

"Sure you did. And I," Breezy pointed at her chest. "Am the next top model."

Jozlyn tilted her head to the side. "You're definitely pretty enough to be a model."

"Flattery will get you everywhere, but seriously. You couldn't have read all those." Breezy inhaled.

"I could and I did. Oh, you don't know. Shoot, listen it's no big deal or anything. It's like this. I look at things, words, or pictures and my mind sort of catalogues everything I see. My brain then processes it and memorizes it. My mom said I've always been that way, but my first memory of being able to do the whole commit to memory word for word was when I was two years old. Now, don't give me that look. Here," Jozlyn handed Breezy one of the journals. It was the latest medical one. "Flip through any page and ask me to quote something from it."

The other woman narrowed her eyes, then did as instructed. After the sixth time and three books later, Breezy sat back with an astonished expression. "That's like amazing. How do you like…keep everything contained in your brain? Do you ever feel like you know too much or your about to burst a blood vessel?"

Jozlyn laughed. "No. The mind has a capacity to hold more knowledge than I'll ever amass."

Breezy pointed her finger at Joz. "You, are the smartest chick ever. High five, girl." She held her hand up and waited for Joz to slap palms. "Listen, when we have trivia night, you are so on my team. Deal?"

Feeling like she found another person who didn't think she was a freak, Joz grinned. "Deal." Joz ran her palms over her arms, a chill stealing over her.

"The guys are back," Breezy exclaimed.

Joz looked at the other woman, wondering how she knew then her mind stopped thinking and locked on the gorgeous form of Turo walking toward her. Lord, did the man have swagger. She'd heard other girls talk about men and their walks and being able to tell a lot about them by that alone. Well, if she was reading him correctly, he certainly had one thing on his mind. The same thing she did.

Getting in his arms and away from the scent of antiseptic.

When he was an arm's length away from her, he paused. "Damn, you sure are a sight for sore eyes. Come here," he said, waiting for her to move the last few feet.

Like a moth to a flame, she went. "I was so worried. Did you…find Jenna?"

Turo tucked her against him. "Yeah, she's with her family."

There was something to his tone that had her tilting her head back. Sadness and lingering anger reflected back at her. "Is she…okay?"

One big hand palmed the back of her head, the other held her around the waist, molding them together from chest to knees. "She will be. You ready to go home?"

With a nod, she tried to step away. "Where are you going?"

She laughed. "I need to grab my things."

He grunted but let her take a step away. "I need to check in with Kellen. Meet you back here in five. Will that give you enough time to do whatever you need?"

Jozlyn checked to see where Breezy was, unable to see the other woman, she shrugged. "I'm not on the clock or anything. I guess I can leave a note for Breezy."

A smile tipped Turo's beautiful lips. Goodness, the man should be illegal. "Don't worry about her. Xan is *practicing* making babies with her, I'm sure, even as we speak. It's getting to the point I feel as though I need to draw that boy a picture." The last was said a bit loud, but Joz was having a hard time imagining the pretty blonde going off to have sex while she worked, even if her boyfriend was extremely good looking.

"What's put that puzzled expression on your gorgeous face?" Turo placed his forefinger under her chin.

She shook her head. "I just can't imagine Breezy…you know, going off to do that with Xan."

"My eyes...my eyes," Coti yelled running out of the breakroom. "Isn't there a rule against banging on the counter in public?"

Turo burst into laughter. "So says the man who has a hard time keeping his dick in his pants on the regular."

Jozlyn looked from the door he'd come out of back to Coti. "Are you pulling my leg?"

"Step through that door, and you'll find out. Heck, you'll get an education on something you might never come back from."

The other man's eyes were like saucers.

"Coti, keep an eye on Joz while I check in with Kellen, will you?" Turo met the other man's laughing gaze.

"Absolutely. We'll play a game. Have you ever played name the dick game?" Coti sat on the counter staring down at Joz.

His mate stared at him then back at Coti? "You mean like what guys call his, or what it's technically called?

Coti rolled his eyes. "Clearly not the technical term. Okay, rules are you can't call it penis, 'cause that's boring as shit. I'll start. Fuckpole extraordinaire. Your turn."

Joz bit her lip. "Beaver Cleaver."

Turo left as Coti hooted with laughter and called out Lincoln log. When he returned it was to hear his friend grousing because he was losing in the name game to Joz.

"I don't believe she's never played before. Seriously, she's a ringer." Coti hopped down from his spot. "She needs to go. I can't have a woman beating me at my own game." His finger was pointing at the door like the angry monkey from Family Guy. "I mean, who says Meat Thermometer when talking about their junk?"

Joz laughed, wiping tears as she grabbed Turo's hand. "You realize he's certifiable, right?"

"Third Leg of the tripod. Beat that," Coti yelled.

"Ignore him. Let's go. I believe I promised you answers." Turo grabbed her hand, steering her away from the door where Coti had pointed.

"Lead the way."

Turo felt like a kid with his first girl as he helped Joz into his truck. Did shifters have heart attacks? His was pounding as he rounded the hood of his vehicle. He took a moment to steady his breathing before climbing in. "You ready?"

Joz adjusted the seatbelt, pulling it down so it didn't hit quite so high on her chest. He made a mental note to do that for her next time he put her into his rig.

"Yep," she answered with a breathy whisper.

His cock jerked beneath the zipper of his jeans. He had to remind himself to hold back, knowing his little mate didn't know about other species such as his. Hell, he didn't even know how to explain about vampires and the hybrids that came from mixing the two, let alone what Jenna was. Taking a deep breath, he reached for her hand, placing their joined fingers on his thigh. The Goddess wouldn't have given him a mate who couldn't or wouldn't accept him for what he was.

"You hungry?" They passed a gas station on their way out of town with only one restaurant before they began the trek to his home. If she wanted something fast, it was her last chance.

Joz shook her head. "We just ate before you guys showed up."

He squeezed her hand, keeping them connected during the drive. Neither of them said a word after they left the city limits. The radio playing was the only noise, both seemingly content. He'd never been one to enjoy the company of many, but with Joz, her presence soothed out all his jagged edges. Mate, the word in and of itself made complete sense to him in that moment. The other half of a pair. One without the other isn't whole. For him, he had been a half being for hundreds of years until he'd found Jozlyn. If she couldn't accept what fate had deemed them to be, he'd not be able to go on. No, Turo realized his life would not be worth living as a half man or wolf any longer, if he didn't have Jozlyn as his mate.

"Hey, what is it?"

He looked down to see he'd been squeezing their combined hands. "Oh, Goddess, tell me I didn't hurt you?"

She placed her other hand over theirs. "No, your hand was shaking really bad. Did you get hurt today?"

He felt her eyes searching his body, looking for wounds. Turo could've told her his only wounds would be internal…that only she held the true power to hurt him, but held his tongue. "I'm fine as you can see. We're here," he said lifting his chin to indicate the driveway leading to his home.

"You're a stubborn fool, Arturo. You know you can tell me anything, and I won't judge you." Her hand wiggled out of his.

Turo opened his senses, checking that all was clear around his property. Jozlyn's safety was the most important thing in the world to him. "Wait 'til

I explain it all to you then I'll ask you to keep an open mind and heart."

One of his garage doors slid open as he pressed the button. He drove in, shutting the door back down once they were fully inside, turning the truck off before the big bay shut completely. He looked around the interior of the large space, searching for anything out of place. As nothing triggered his wolf, he exhaled then got out on his side. Walking around to the passenger side, he opened the door for Joz and helped her down. His little mate rolled her eyes but came right into his waiting arms. "I like holding you," he murmured into the dark fall of her hair.

"I've noticed." She wrapped her arms around his shoulders.

At the keypad to his home, Turo shifted Jozlyn so he could enter the code. His eyes widened as she punched in the code. His inner alarms went off then calmed as he realized his mate or soon to be mate should know all his secrets, including his security measures. "Do you have the codes memorized for my safe room as well?"

She bit her bottom lip. "I don't do it intentionally."

He rubbed his nose against hers. "Of course you don't. It's like breathing to you, isn't it?"

"Yes," she said on a deep exhale. "I usually try to turn away, or do something else so I don't accidentally stumble upon things of a private nature, but I was too intrigued by what you were going to show me."

They were walking through his home to the living area while she talked. He sat her down gently on the big sofa. "Hahai, you don't need to give me privacy. After I tell you about me and my...past, you'll understand more. However, I'm going to need you to keep an open mind. Can you do that?"

Jozlyn nodded, folding her hands in front of her.

Turo walked away then came to sit on the large piece of wood he'd carved himself that served as a coffee table. "I'm sure you've noticed some strange things about me and the other members of the Iron Wolves, right?"

She nodded but kept quiet.

261

Taking a deep breath, Turo held out his hand. "We are more than human, Joz. Me and your friends, Lyric, Syn, Laikyn and even Breezy. We are shifters, created by mixing Fey with human. No, don't be afraid." He put his hand on her leg as she shifted away. "Look, I know you think I'm crazy, but I can prove it." With his hand still extended, he allowed his claws to grow and hair to form. Most of the younger shifters couldn't shift one part of their body at a time, except maybe Kellen.

A gasp escaped Jozlyn. "What do you turn into?"

He could hear her heart beating. The erratic pounding had him shifting back to full human. "We're wolves."

Her throat worked to swallow before she tried to speak again. "And Egypt's father...is he one too?"

"Goddess, no," he denied.

"But he's something other, right? One of the patients said he was a monster. What exactly is he? I've sort of been living in this bubble, going through the motions like everything was normal, but it's not.

Tell me all of it. I mean, I'm probably fired for absconding with a patient, especially since the patient in question's father is clearly not human. Now…you're not what I thought you were. Oh God, how am I supposed to explain this to my mother?"

Turo growled, making Joz scoot away from him. "Dammit, I'm fucking this up. You're safer with me than you'll ever be. I'd give my life for yours, Joz. Trust me on that if nothing else. As for Egypt's father, yes, he's a monster, the worst sort." Turo took a deep breath. "He's a vampire. One who's taken the blood of a shifter, which gives him the ability to walk during the day. The reason the woman said he was a monster is because some vampires aren't satisfied unless they kill the humans they feed off of. When they do that, they literally begin rotting from the inside out. Kenneth found Asia, who was his mate. Her blood slowed the process down for him, but he still continued to kill humans. He's a sick and twisted bastard."

Joz sat in silence, a stunned look of disbelief on her beautiful features.

"You don't believe me." He nodded. "Open your mind to mine. Let me show you." He would white wash some of the horrors, but his little mate needed to see the truth for herself.

"What do you mean?" She blinked red rimmed eyes. He hated seeing his strong woman on the verge of tears.

"You have the mind of a genius and have walls so thick around it I can't enter it. We, as shifters are able to communicate telepathically. Do you meditate?"

Joz nodded.

"Good, I want you to try and relax, listen to my voice. I swear to you, I will never hurt you or allow anyone else to do so." He sat with his legs bracketing hers, his large palms resting on her thighs. He counted that a step in the right direction. Slowly, he began walking her through the meditation for beginners. Although she'd said she meditated, he wanted her to focus on his voice and follow where he led, opening her Chakra and allowing him into her head. Fifteen minutes later, a small door opened in her mind, welcoming him in. Instead of going through, he motioned her forward, showing her what she needed to see through his memories.

Jozlyn couldn't believe the vastness of Turo's knowledge. Lord, the man was so much more than he showed the world. The images that they ghosted past, she filed away for further examination at a later time. Finally, when they reached a door with a pulsating red energy, she knew without asking these were the most recent memories, the ones that would forever change her life. Squaring her shoulders, she allowed Turo to lead her through. Inside, she watched as Turo and a group of men divided up. She recognized Xan and the other men as they stepped out of the big tank like vehicle next to Turo's. As their bodies morphed into large wolves, she put her hand over her mouth, holding the gasp in.

They were beautiful animals as they raced into the woods. She wasn't sure if this was something Turo had seen or if he was showing her what they were. However, the scene changed again to Turo and his crew walking into a home. The scents that assailed her were the most obnoxious she'd ever smelled. Immediately she reached up to plug her nose but noticed the men didn't seem to pay any attention, or if they did, they had a purpose and stayed focused on it. As her eyes adjusted to the darkness, she wondered why there was shadows throughout, but then Turo was dragging her down the stairs. Something had her trying to pull back, but the vision didn't relent. As if in slow motion, she saw a horror show come to life, with six real life blood sucking men waiting for them.

As Turo and his team began shooting, killing the beings, Joz was like a bystander taking it all in without notice. Her eyes stayed glued as Turo killed one thing after another, their eyes blood red as they tried to reach him.

Finally, he walked her through the door of his mind to a field. "You're safe, breathe, hahai," Turo whispered over and over.

Joz didn't realize she wasn't until his words penetrated the fog surrounding her. "They're real," she said.

"Yes," he agreed.

"Where are we now?" She asked, looking at the soft ground they were sitting on.

Turo's eyes lit up. "This was one of my favorite places as a kid."

She could hear the sound of water. "Are you originally from Hawaii?"

He shrugged. "I'm hundreds of years old, hahai. It wasn't called that when I was younger. However, I always loved it here. I try to come back at least once a year to recharge, even if it's in my dreams. What do you think?"

Joz stood, and he noticed her legs had a tremor to them. "Show me what you look like when you shift."

He knew she was going to ask to see his wolf, but he'd thought she'd give him…them more time. "I don't want to scare you, little one."

She snorted. "You just showed me a living horror show. Pretty sure I can handle you turning into a wolf. Besides, I saw Xan and the others do it."

He'd purposefully showed her the others shifting, thinking it would ease her curiosity. With a sigh, he too stood. "Alright, but remember, I'm still me in my other form. I can communicate with you through our mental link, if you permit it." Hell, only those who were really strong could keep him out. Those like her, dammit.

Now, standing before his fated mate, he nodded. "Alright, but not here."

Turo brought them out of the meditative state gently. His large living area was made of natural materials, things he'd bought purposefully so his home was an extension of the outside. Moving the large coffee table closer to the bay window, he cleared the space between the sofa and the stone fireplace. "I can do this several ways. A swift change where I'm man and then wolf, or slowly. Which would you prefer?" He was putting the power in her hands.

"You mean like...in the movies where it looks and sounds painful? No, thank you. Just get naked and become wolf, please." She'd pulled her legs up to her chest, making herself appear tiny.

He didn't want to tell her that since Jenna had showed up, they'd learned how to tap into their heritage more and no longer needed to remove their clothing to shift. Of course, if they were in a hurry, or desperate times, then all bets were off on whether they'd remember to think away their clothing. With his gaze holding hers, he pulled is T-shirt over his head, dropping it onto the floor by his feet. His boots were kicked off then shoved to the side. Keeping a firm hold on his beast, he unsnapped the top button on his jeans, working the denim down his legs along with his briefs, leaving him standing naked in front of his mate.

"Holy crap." She covered her mouth with her hand. "Um, yeah, that's an impressive package. Continue," she ordered.

His wry chuckle escaped before he could stop it. "Yes, ma'am." The change flowed over him quickly. One moment he was on two legs then he was on four, seeing things through the eyes of his wolf. Trotting over to the couch, he sniffed Jozlyn. In his shifted form, everything was magnified, even her honeysuckle sweet scent. He licked her palm as she lifted it, making her giggle.

Laying his head on her lap, he let her pet him.

"You're so soft," she whispered.

He snorted but was sure it came out a strange chuff. Stepping away, he shifted back and grabbed up his jeans. The denim slid over his sensitive skin while she kept her eyes locked on him.

"Say something." He pulled the coffee table back and took a seat in the same spot he'd been earlier.

"Do you want me to scream, or should I be passing out or something like that?" She unfolded her legs and stood.

His wolf snarled inside. He didn't like the idea of either of those options. "No. What do you feel?" She was his...everything. Mate, female, woman, whatever you wanted to call it, Fate had decided they were the perfect halves of one whole. Without her, he couldn't live, wouldn't be able to go on. Others could say what they wanted, but a man couldn't survive without his heart.

"I don't know, but I know you're a good man, no matter what you can change into. Those other things, they're not." She swallowed. "Will they be coming after me?"

He swept her into his arms, the thought of anyone touching her, harming her had him growling low. "Not as long as there's breath in my body." Lowering his head, giving her plenty of time to push him away, he dipped his head down, pressing his lips against hers, kissing her with every fiber of his being behind it, allowing her to feel everything he felt for her. The kiss started slow, built to an intensity that quickly became more.

Her arms circled his head, holding him to her as her legs wrapped around his hips. His woman returned his kiss with as much vigor as he gave. In the far recess of his brain, he thought he should slow down, but the only thing he wanted to do was bury himself inside his sweet mate.

"I want to make love to you," he groaned against her lips.

"Yes," she whispered, pulling his head back down to hers.

Needing no further encouragement, Turo took them back to his bedroom, stumbling as he tripped over his boots. "Shit," he exclaimed.

"Am I too heavy for you, tiger?" Jozlyn joked.

Turo kicked the boot out of his way then bit his mate's lip, tasting the sweet coppery flavor, soothing the slight hurt with his tongue. "You're a sassy one. I'll have to remember that." He laid her on his bed, his body ready to take and to hell with any preliminaries. "Need you naked, hahai."

The scent of her arousal washed over him, making his dick jerk behind the fly of his jeans. He hissed. "You've got way too many clothes on as do I. Wanna race and see who can get naked first?"

"Seeing as you're down to one article of clothing, I don't think that's a fair race. How about you help me out of mine." She played with the end of the scrub top, giving him a peek at her abdomen.

Turo lifted the shirt over her head. Her dark hair having a bit of static electricity to it, had strands standing out all over it. He ran his palms over the softness, down over her shoulder and sides, making her giggle. She laughed huskily, the sound making his dick even harder as she shimmied out of the bottoms. Lying in nothing but skin, he swore he'd never seen anything sexier.

He could see each inhale and exhale as she tried to pretend a calmness she didn't feel. The vision she created with her hard-tipped nipples could bring any man to his knees, and Turo was sure his dick was ready to come at the sight. Something he had never done in all his years. Fuck. This little bit of a human was undoing his self-control.

He bent, his gaze focused on the flesh between her thighs. His wolf whimpered, wanting to taste, but he pushed the animal side back. Turo took hold of her breasts plumping them in his palms. They were small but perfect.

A hiss escaped as he bent and took one puckered nipple into his mouth. He found her other breast with his free hand, cupping and squeezing as he licked and sucked the twin. "You're so unbelievably sexy, Joz, fucking, perfect," he said, continuing his assault on her breasts as he switched between the twin globes.

Jozlyn tugged on his hair. "I want to see you again."

He stared at her puzzled then realized what she wanted. His dick pulsed with each beat of his heart, digging into the zipper of his jeans. Climbing off the bed, he stepped back and pulled the sides away, careful he didn't catch anything important in the teeth of his zipper. He hissed as his cock was freed from the restraints and stared down as Joz moved forward on her hands and knees.

"You really are big."

"Not too big," he grinned.

She licked her lower lip then bit it. "I'm not a virgin, but I'm not a hundred percent sure that is gonna fit in my hooha." She pointed from his dick to her pussy.

He moved up and over her, shoving her onto her back quickly. "Trust me, Jozlyn, you were made for me." He kissed her, letting her feel everything he'd held back from other women for years. All the pent-up emotions, the knowledge that she was the only woman who would complete him, he poured into the kiss and through the link they'd forged in his living room. His tongue plunged in and out of her mouth the way his body ached to do.

She whimpered, and he worried he'd hurt her. "Are you okay?"

Tears were in her eyes. "You...you think you love me?"

Turo wiped away the wetness from under her eyes. "Jozlyn, I know it's new to you, but when we find our mates, something clicks inside us. My soul knows yours. I would do anything for you, even walk away if that's what you wanted." It would kill him, but he'd do it. He pushed up on his arms, not wanting to do anything she didn't want.

Jozlyn's hands were between them, shoving the final covering away from his body. Then, her hand was stroking up and down his erection, making him weak with relief. His resolve to leave her shattered. "Final chance, hahai. If you don't want me, us, tell me now. Once I have you I'll mate you, mark you, make you mine for always," he warned. He'd waited several lifetimes for his mate. Fate brought him a human who was too delicate, too young, and too good, but he'd be damned if he allowed her to leave him once he had her.

"I want you. I know what that means. I was in your mind a lot more than what you showed me, Arturo Anoa'i. I saw you and your hundreds of years. Yes, it's going to take me a little bit to filter it all, but I know you. I know what's in your heart, and...I want us." She touched him, smoothing her hand up and down his dick. "Make us one," she whispered.

Her words had him bending to her mouth. His hands shook as he braced them next to her head. He took great care as he eased over her completely, keeping his eyes locked on her face. He knew he should do more than just enter her this first time, but his primal beast wanted in her now. Her hand stroking him was making it impossible to think of anything except fucking into her. Then, her wide-eyed look and words of worry about him fitting had him shifting so he could move his hand down her stomach. Her muscles contracted as he reached the soft patch of hair between her thighs.

He silenced her with his mouth as he let his finger trail through her wetness. She squirmed beneath him as he parted her folds and rubbed her clit, using her juices, bringing excited gasps from her parted lips. One finger slid into her incredible tightness, then another as he worked her into a hard and fast orgasm.

She was so fucking tight as her pussy contracted around his two digits he didn't think there was any way she'd be able to take his cock, not unless he worked a little harder.

Moving down her body, he stared at the beautiful being who was his. Her fingers twisted in the sheets as he moved her legs apart and made a spot for himself. Inhaling he took in her sweet perfume of arousal and knew he'd never tire of the scent. With expert fingers, he spread her slit, finding her pretty pink pussy coated with more of her cream, and he nearly came right then and there.

With a snarl, Turo lowered his head and pressed a kiss to the top of her mound then licked from top to bottom and back, circling her opening. Goddess, she tasted even better than his favorite sweets. A temptation he'd never be able to go for long periods without tasting.

He thrust his tongue into her as she cried out. Her legs lifted, clamping around his head. Turo laughed then slid his arms under her ass and held her to him, keeping her in place as he fucked her with his tongue. Jozlyn tried to squirm in his hold, but the only thing it did was rub her against him, making her pussy spasm. Her breathing grew rapidly louder.

"Oh, Turo," she cried!

Her sweet cream flooded his mouth, and he took it all, swallowing it like a starved man, needing, wanting more. The temptation to mark her right then and there rode him, but he wanted to be buried balls deep the first time he sank his canines into her. Letting go of one perfect ass cheek, he pressed two fingers inside, testing her readiness then added a third, stretching her for him. His need was almost to the point he'd disgrace himself by blowing his load as soon as the head of his dick entered her.

A quick look up had him seeing Joz staring down at him then her hips rose to meet his face, a silent demand he was more than happy to oblige. Increasing the motion of his fingers, he brought his mouth down on her clit and sucked, hard. She cried out. Her legs shook as the walls of her pussy constricted around his pumping fingers.

She went limp, but he was far from done.

Turo moved up and over her again, parting her legs with his. "Joz, you okay?" He held his cock in his hand, lining up to his very own paradise, her entrance.

Joz's dark gaze met his, and she smiled. "Make me yours, Turo."

"You already are. This is just the dot at the end of the first sentence. You've been mine since you took your first breath, and I'll be yours 'til I take my last." He couldn't control the tremble that shook him, as he slid the tip of his dick into Joz. "From this point on, we are one, Joz. You and me. You completed me, made me whole again."

Joz reached up and caressed his cheek, a dampness he didn't know had escaped from his tightly closed eyes, and he would swear it was sweat she wiped off. "That's the most beautiful thing I've ever heard, Turo. Make love to me."

He pushed forward, her tightness scorching him, but he held still while she adjusted to his invasion. Finally, he was in his mate. All was as it should be. Now the only thing left was to mark her, so the world knew she was his. Once her body no longer fought his, he began easing in and out, using all his knowledge and strength to bring her with him.

His wolf howled, wanting to mark their mate, but he wanted to make it last. Heck, he wasn't sure if he'd explained about the marking to Joz, and then there was no more thinking as his body took over.

Sweat slick bodies moved together, hers welcoming his as he moved in and then trying to hold him as he moved out. The harder and faster he moved, the more she urged him on with moans.

"Goddess, you feel so fucking good. Can't hold out much longer. Need you to come," he grunted between slams of his body into hers.

Her nails raked down his back. "Yes, oh, yes, right there." She swiveled her hips.

He raised her right leg over his hip and powered into her harder, faster. "Come for me," he ordered.

Her body tightened around him, as she found her release. He gritted his teeth, and then, he couldn't fight it anymore, pounding in and out until he poured into her.

Jozlyn squirmed under him. "More, need more."

Goddess, yes. He smiled, bending and taking her lips in a kiss. Hoping she could take more, he pumped his hips, giving her all of himself as he settled fully inside her once more, knowing she was his heaven. "You okay?"

The urge to mark her, bite her was there even more. He held back resisting the urge. She lifted against him, pressing her hips up, taking all of him inside her. "Hurts so good."

He feathered kisses over her brow, her nose, and then her mouth, loving the oneness of it all. Any other time he'd been with a woman, he'd never had this connection.

Her eyes narrowed. "Are you thinking of other women?"

"No…I mean." He held still, being balls deep inside your mate was the last place you should ever think of another. "I was thinking how perfect it felt to be here that I'd never had this before. I was barely alive before you, and that's the truth."

Joz's legs wrapped around him, squeezing and thrusting her hips she demanded he move.

He found he had no more willpower than to give into what they both needed and wanted, moving in and out of her velvety depths, kissing a trail from her lips to her neck. "I want to mark you here. Did you see that in my memories as well?" he whispered gruffly.

She tilted her head, giving him access while her mind opened. Goddess, she had as much knowledge in her young life as he did in his long one. Her easy acceptance floored him. Never had he thought to be blessed with such a treasure, never thought he'd know such bliss.

A moan came from her right before he licked, her words sealing them. "Mine," she said.

He felt his canines burst from his gums, and there was no holding him or his wolf back. "Mine," he agreed before sinking his teeth into her neck.

Turo was sure light exploded all around them as their souls began weaving together by invisible bonds. He only allowed a small amount of her blood to coat his tongue, enough to bind them and mark her as his before he pulled free, sealing the wound with his tongue.

His cock continued to pump in and out of her, her pussy constricting from the release she'd had from his bite. Pleasure washed over him at the knowledge she was his forever. If he looked closely enough, he was sure he could see clear into her soul. As his gaze came back into focus, he found her unsteady gaze staring at him and smiled. "You're mine forever now."

She was panting, her nails going up and down his back. "You realize that's a two-way street, right?"

He looked down at her puzzled. "What's that?"

"You're mine too. Um, so when do you make me like you?" she asked with her dark hair fanning out around her like a soft cloud.

He stilled. "You know about that?"

Joz laughed, running her foot down his leg and back up, making his dick twitch inside her. "I was in your head. I saw a lot more than what you showed me. Remember, super brain here."

Most men would've been scared shitless at the knowledge their mate knew all their secrets, but not him. He took satisfaction and pride in knowing Jozlyn would never be left in the dark, or be one of those women he'd worry couldn't handle what was thrown at her.

"Did you see inside mine as well?" she asked.

Turo eased out of her, her slight wince had him moving slower. He glanced down at the mark he'd left on her neck. "I didn't. Not until you give me permission."

She pulled him down and held him tight. "You have my permission. Now, about the rest…when and how. What about my parents?"

Chapter Thirteen

Jozlyn wondered at the panicked look on Turo's face. "Remember complete honesty here, Arturo."

A muscle in his jaw twitched as he sat up on the side of the bed. Suddenly she felt cold lying naked without him covering her. "Don't look at me like that, hahai," he said.

Pulling herself into a sitting position, she grabbed the sheet and covered herself. "Alright, explain."

Turo glanced at her then away. "Your parents will continue to age as humans do, but as you already know or should from what I told you…I'm not, we're not…" He stopped and took a deep breath. "Shifters are created differently than humans. Yes, we have human DNA as well, but the Fey gifted us with theirs as well, giving us longevity. Most of the other shifters live long into their hundreds. I'm over three hundred years old, Jozlyn."

She stared at his back, listening to him. "Alright, so my parents can't know that their future son-in-law is older than dirt."

"This is nothing to joke about. You can't tell your parents about our dual nature. We live in secrecy for a reason. Imagine if the government found out about us. It's why we live in packs, and most of us don't have public lives for the most part. The MC, we keep the public away. It's been that way for centuries. I've travelled the world and lived within other shifter communities from time to time. It has never been any different. I've also lived in the human society, passing as a normal human, but they knew something about me was different. We can't cage our wolves for long. We need the woods to shift and run. A pack is where safety lies. If your parents knew they'd shit a brick. Maybe they'd confide to their closest friend, who would then tell their friend and so on."

Joz snorted. "You don't know my parents yet, wait to make any sort of assumptions until you do. Heck, I'm not even sure what my dad does, to be honest. I mean, I don't think he does anything illegal or anything," she laughed as Turo glared over his shoulder at her.

"What do you mean, you don't know what he does?" His arm came over her legs.

Her eyes went to between his legs, watching as his dick jerked. "Maybe you should…cover that." She waved toward his growing erection.

Turo's grin was wicked. "Nah, he'd just protest the confinement." The he in question jerked up and down.

"Oh my god, are you doing that on purpose? Can you make him dance, too?" She reached her hand out to encircle him, feeling the left-over wetness from their lovemaking. Many would think it was gross, but she loved the memory of having him inside her.

"Woman, you're too sore for much more of that," he groaned.

His face was inches from hers, the dark orbs flashed to an electric blue. "They change," she gasped her hand stilling on his hardness.

"What?" His hand covering her smaller one.

"Your eyes. I thought I was seeing things before, but sometimes, like now, they turn blue."

Turo's forehead touched hers. "It's my wolf. He's dominant, but I hold him in check for the most part. I don't want to be alpha. I respect Kellen and his position. Xan is his second, which is a good choice. I like where I'm at."

She looked at his features, wondering what he meant, then something tugged at her memory. "A hierarchy. The pack has one. You're an enforcer. Isn't that dangerous?"

He shrugged. "Life for shifters has always been dangerous. More so in the last year or so."

File after file she flipped through what she'd stored during her trip through his mind, reading through his memories quickly. "Oh my god, Lyric was almost killed and Laikyn too. Why didn't I know my friends…I could've almost lost them?" she cried.

Turo moved quickly, rolling them to the side, holding her close to his chest. "Kellen and Rowan would move heaven and earth to protect their mates, just as I would for you. You are safer now than you have ever been."

"That doesn't solve the problem of my parents. They'll know if I'm hiding something from them, not to mention the fact I won't age a bit in thirty or forty years. Don't you think they might recognize that?" She propped herself up against his chest, their legs tangling as she watched the expressions flit across his features. Her mate was beauty personified. Oh, he was all man and would hate to know she thought him beautiful, but he was.

"Jenna can help with that. She's the Fey Queen." Turo ran his hand down her back, his calluses a delicious caress, as he cupped her ass and moved her closer to his thigh. "Now, about your dad?"

"Um, slow your roll, big guy. Fey Queen? Explain, sir." She tried to hold still as he continued to run that big hand up and down, teasing between the cheeks of her ass, but damn, did it feel good.

"Hmm, did I not tell you about that? Jennaveve is the Fey Queen. She comes from a different realm, where things are totally different. It's why your friend's pregnancy was so quick. Time is fluid there. A month here, could be three or four days there. We don't really know how to calculate it, only know the women went there while we handled the threats here, and bam, babies were almost ready to pop. Trust me, both Kellen and Rowan were not prepared to see their wives waddling when they went to retrieve their mates."

She sat up, the sheet falling away. "Wait, you mean this other world is like ours, but time like flies by, or is it a parallel only changing in between as you return?"

Turo groaned. "You want to know the particulars, don't you?"

Joz couldn't help but grin. He sounded pained. "It's the thirst for knowledge. It gets me excited."

Her mate pumped his hand up and down his dick. "I thought I could do that for you."

She glanced down at his hand, watching as a bead of pearly fluid appeared. "Well, you certainly are pretty high up on there too. I think I need a little more knowledge on this whole mating thing. You up for another tutorial, Mr. Anoa'i?"

Joz rose up, tossing the sheet away from them and wrapped her hand around the base of his cock, stroking him from root to tip with one hand. She scooted down, never letting go of that monster he seemed to think of as another entity. Of course, if she had another body part as large as the one she was stroking, she'd surely feel the same way. "My, what big…balls you have," she whispered as she curled her other palm around the large globes, making him moan.

"Woman, you're killing me here." Turo fisted his hand in her hair, moving the heavy mass back, giving him a view of what she was about to do.

She looked up the length of his tanned body then back down at the mushroomed head of his dick. The pearly drop beckoned her. Dipping her tongue into the small slit, she couldn't contain her own moan of pleasure as his flavor filled her mouth. His hand flexed in her hair, demanding she move on him.

Never in her life had she felt the urge to do what she was, but with Turo it was as natural as breathing.

"Straddle my leg, hahai," Turo ordered.

His words didn't make sense until he shifted to help her do as he said. The first contact her clit had with his hair roughened thigh made her cry out. Lord love the man and his ingenious ways.

She licked over the head once more, taking more of him inside until she felt confident she could slide at least half his cock in without gagging. Turo's grip on her hair helped move her in the motion he needed, and she knew he was racing toward completion. His thigh shifted, hitting her clit, making her pussy clench and her toes curl. She groaned around the dick in her mouth, worried she'd come before he did. Tightening her hand around the base, while squeezing his balls, she worked him harder, sucking and licking, letting him show her how fast he wanted her to go.

Turo's hips flexed beneath her as she bobbed her head, trying to keep up with his fast, hard rhythm. She groaned around him, feeling her impending orgasm racing toward her. She rolled her own hips, wanting to go over the edge but not before Turo.

"Baby, I'm right there. Tell me now if you don't want to..." He yelled as she sucked harder, pumping her hand and twisting it around his shaft. Turo roared as his pleasure hit, his come filling her mouth.

Jozlyn moaned around his dick as he shouted her name, his fingers tightening almost to the point of pain as he pushed her even farther on his cock than she'd taken him before. She breathed out of her nose, feeling him bump the back of her throat as she swallowed as much of his orgasm as she could. With each pulse and flex of the cock in her mouth, it triggered the same reaction in her own body, making her groan around Turo's length.

Turo pulled her off him. "Damn, hahai, I'm sorry. I lost control." He pulled her up and flipped them so she was lying under him, worry creasing his brow.

His breathing was hard and rapid as his eyes shifted to her neck. "Do it, mark me again." Joz didn't know why, but she wanted that bite. Only a second passed, and then, Turo licked the spot before she felt the bite of his fangs. Tingles raced over her as he sucked, setting off another mini orgasm. When he finished, gently withdrawing, she wished she could mark him as well.

"You can and will, hahai." Turo brushed the hair out of her face. "I've bitten you twice now. You'll become like me. Like us. Kellen will be your alpha, since I'm part of his pack. Usually it takes a few days, but when Lyric bit Rowan he turned pretty quickly. He was an unusual case, though. However, I've bitten you twice. There's something different about you that I can't put my finger on."

Joz stared up at Turo. "Lyric bit Rowan?"

Turo shook his head. "Is that all you got out of what I just said?" His mate's mind was a complex thing he'd never understand. Even now, he tried to see what she was thinking, but it was like looking at a mathematician's graph. Oh, he had no doubt in time he'd be able to work through her thought process.

Joz raised her right hand, running her thumb between his brows. "I understand I'll be able to do what you do. Shift, grow fangs, and become all hairy like a wolf. I'm hoping I can be a vegan wolf since I don't see myself being able to…you know hunt Peter Cottontail."

Groaning, he rolled them until she was lying on top of him. "What is up with you humans and your fairy tales?"

She wiggled until she sat on top him. "Whatever do you mean?"

He held her still, knowing he would hurt her if he tried to fuck her again so soon. "Rowan's first thought when he found out about shifters was Bambi."

His mate's entrance into his mind shocked him at the ease with which she did so. He allowed her to see the memory he was talking about and laughed with her as she saw the hilarity in the situation. "So, Rowan is like you now? No wonder he was all growly around us and Harlow. Oh, so can the babies shift? Holy shit, are they…cubs instead of babies?"

Turo laughed. "Stop overthinking things. We're mostly humanish. I mean, we have longer lives, can shift into wolves, and have the ability to speak telepathically, but we fuck like humans, have normal children who learn to shift as well. No, they don't come out as wolves, although we'd love them if they did. Now, on the Fey realm, all bets are off on what is there. I think that's something you should learn another day. For now, are you hungry?" His stomach chose that moment to rumble.

"I could definitely eat something. For clarity, I'm not a vegetarian as you know. I mean, bacon," she laughed.

"You have a thing for bacon, I gather?" He sat up, taking her with him as he stood and placed her on her feet.

Jozlyn nodded, looking around the floor. "Bacon is like the food of the gods."

He tried to see what she was looking for. "What is it?" he asked.

"Where's my clothes?"

Bending he kissed her on the forehead. "Why don't you wear one of my T-shirts? It'll fit you more like a dress and please me to see you in something of mine."

A red blush stole over his mate's body. "Also, easy access for you?"

He grinned, showing off his most wolfish smile. "Well, there is that. But, it's too soon for any more of that for now. Let's go feed another appetite. I'm not sure when your wolf will show up. If you start feeling anything, let me know." He pulled a white T-shirt from his closet, as he spoke, helping Joz put it on. "I enjoy the taking off much better than the putting on."

She grinned up at him. "This smells like you though." She lifted the front up to her nose.

"You can smell me? Is that new or the same as before?"

"I don't know. Since I've met you, there's always been an awareness, but we've sort of skipped over a lot of the usual dating rituals." Her shoulder lifted in a negligent shrug.

He worried she was upset at missing what all women wanted. The courting. Date nights. Things he hadn't given her. Hell, he'd only brought her danger and life altering changes.

"Don't," she admonished. "I was involved in the Iron Wolves before I met you to a certain extent thanks to my friendship with the girls. Egypt was…is my patient. I kinda brought danger to your door."

Her mind was completely open to him, allowing him to see what she was feeling and thinking. He thought on that then shook his head. "No, fate had a way of making sure we found our way to each other. You were in my mind. You saw I was leaving, thinking it was in your best interest. Fate had me stopping at that cabin in the woods to find Asia. Don't you think it was more than just coincidence that she was your patient's mama?" He watched as she processed his words then a smile lit up her face.

"So, you're saying you wouldn't have gotten very far before coming back?" Her eyes wouldn't meet his.

The sound of insecurity didn't set well with him or his wolf. "Jozlyn, I have searched for centuries for you. When I saw you with Lyric, I knew you were mine, but I thought you were too young for me. Look at you." He waved his hand up and down her petite body. "You're everything I'm not. Soft, sweet, perfect in every single way. I'm so far on the opposite side of good I fear I will taint you.

She put her hand over his heart, her own beating rapidly. "No, quit saying that. If what you say is true then you are exactly as you see me, and what I see is the best man ever. You went into a lone cabin and risked your life for a stranger. You then brought her back to your family, risking not only your life, but theirs as well to save her, not knowing she was intertwined in my life. You did all that unselfishly, so don't give me that line of bullcrap. You'd do it again tomorrow if you found another human or…other in need. Now, feed me mate." She stood on her toes stopping him from answering.

Never one to argue with his mate, especially when she was pressing against him and making his heart feel lighter than it had in hundreds of years, Turo kissed her back. Before they could take the sweet press of lips into a more carnal one, his mate's stomach growled loudly, making him pull back. "Feed one appetite, then the other."

"What're we making?"

The way she asked, he knew she wouldn't sit back and let him take care of her. Turo realized he was no longer a lone wolf searching for a mate, but a man who had one who would demand he allowed her to run beside him. Goddess, he couldn't wait for her to shift.

Chapter Fourteen

"Can we get my Bug?" Joz asked Turo when they'd finished cleaning up after grilling burgers. She'd explained about her dad's job as a judge and how he travelled all over giving speeches and such. Her mother said he enjoyed talking, and it got him out of the house. It also kept their personal life exciting, but Joz didn't want or need to know those details.

Turo looked up from tossing the last of the garbage away. How the man could eat a half dozen of the largest ones this side of Texas she had no clue, but he did without pausing or blinking. When she'd stared, he'd shrugged and said it was a shifter thing. Of course, she assumed all shifters must have fast metabolisms 'cause none that she'd come across, not even her friends Lyric or Syn, looked as if they needed to watch what they ate.

Turo glanced at her from where he was putting the last dish in the dishwasher; his jaw ticked. "Alright," he said.

She wondered at his hesitancy. "No secrets, remember. What made you pause?"

He shrugged. "I was hoping you'd shift here in the privacy of my property."

"You said Rowan was an exception. How many humans have you seen changed?"

"In all honesty?" She nodded. "I can't remember ever being there to witness any. However, from what I've been told it usually takes a day or two."

Laughing she went up to him, wrapping her arms around his waist. Standing in front of him, she was acutely aware of the difference in their sizes. She loved how much larger he was than her. He made her feel protected and girlie, yet equal. It was a phenomenon she'd never thought she'd have with a man. Heck, she was sure any man who took her on would be inferior in intellect or a total brainiac, which would then make him a douche, in Lyric's words. "So, you thought I'd change in a couple hours 'cause you're some super wolf, or because you willed it so?"

He grinned down at her. "Hey, I am a super wolf." He puffed out his chest and howled.

The human tone made her grin and snuggle into his chest. "It'll happen when it does. Until then, I'd really like to have my car here instead of at the club."

His big arms contracted around her. "Alright, let's do it."

Looking into his dark eyes, she could've sworn they flashed to a sheen of blue before settling back to his dark orbs. The man was fighting his wolf by letting her have her way. She didn't understand why it was so hard for him, but she needed to make sure he knew from the get-go that she was an independent woman. As she moved out of his arms, she felt a small itch beneath the surface of her skin, but hid it from Turo. No way was she going to tell him in case he used it as a reason to not leave. Surely, that small sign meant her wolf was waking up, and it would be another day or so. She really should talk to Rowan, find out what his first sign was.

Her borrowed scrubs had been washed and dried, reminding her she really needed to stop by her house and get some clothes. She'd tackle that with Turo after she got her own car. The man was way too overprotective. Start as you mean to go on her mama always said.

He showed her how he checked the garage and surrounding area for safety by opening his senses through their mind link. Jozlyn was still amazed to connect with him on such a level. Turo seemed to think she could do it because of her complex brain, which she still thought weird, but as they backed out of his garage, she concentrated the way he'd shown her. Nature had its own vibration once you were open to it she recognized. The air smelled earthier to her now. Everything seemed more magnified, but she didn't want to worry Turo as they made their way back toward the club. Surely it wasn't because her wolf was close to emerging.

"You've gone quiet on me. You okay?" Turo placed his big palm on her thigh, squeezing her leg.

His warmth gave her comfort, helping her focus on him instead of the outside. "I'm fine. It's a lot to process." Which wasn't a lie.

"You've handled it quite well. You don't have to do everything at once. You know that's what being pack is about. We lean on each other. Once you shift, you'll be able to link with anyone at any time. I'll show you how to knock on their minds before just popping in. Trust me, it's for the best, especially if you want to visit with Breezy. Xan is a sick bastard," he chuckled.

She turned to look at him, a question in her eyes and waited for an explanation.

"Trust me, that wolf says he's practicing making babies, but he's just a horny ass pup." He made air quotes around the word practicing before returning his hands to the wheel.

"I kinda figured that out when you guys returned yesterday and he dragged Breezy away immediately. Is that legal for him to do when she's at work?"

Turo laughed, the full bellied sound floating through the cab of the pickup. "Sweetheart, you'll see for yourself, wolves have an appetite for a lot more than just food."

The heat in his eyes had an answering one shooting straight to her core. Goodness gracious, she'd already had more orgasms with Turo in one day than she'd had in her entire sex life, and she was even now wishing he would pull over and do it again.

"Damn, whatever you're thinking must be dirty. I can smell your arousal and it's making me fucking hard." His hand moved from her thigh to the apex between her legs, rubbing in a delicious up and down motion.

"If you don't stop, I'm going to have a visible wet spot," she groaned.

"Only fair since I'm going to be sporting a visible hard-on," Turo growled.

Her legs tried to clamp together as she shuddered. "Yeah, but yours can go away, mine will stain these lovely pink scrubs."

His eyes left the road to look at his hand between her thighs. "I'd love to taste you right now."

"Did you hear what I just said. Oh, god." She couldn't stop moving as his hand snaked up and untied her pants. With deft movements, he had his fingers sifting through her wetness. Joz closed her eyes as he pumped two fingers into her, no longer caring if her pants got wet.

"Come for me, Joz. Let me here you scream," he ordered.

Joz could do nothing else as he pumped in and out of her. His palm rubbed her clit with each in and out of his fingers inside her. She closed her eyes, and then as stars exploded behind her eyes, she bit her lip and yelled his name.

The sound of gravel crunching beneath his tires and swerving of the vehicle didn't register until she heard Turo cursing. Opening her eyes, she looked up to see they were on the side of the road and her mate was removing his fingers from her, licking them clean. "You taste like honeysuckle and wine. I could get addicted to you," he said holding her gaze as he stuck both his fingers into his mouth.

"Holy shit, did we almost wreck?" She looked at the steep incline off to the side.

"Nah, I had complete control, but I didn't want to waste one drop of your cream. If I didn't think you'd mind, I'd get out and strip your pants down and lick you right here on the side of the road," he said, promise lacing his voice.

She could feel more of her juices flowing from his words.

"Don't. Don't look at me like that, or I swear I'll not be responsible for public display of fucking."

"Is PDF illegal you think?" Joz looked at the huge bulge in his jeans then back at him.

Turo adjusted his dick in his jeans. "I'm pretty sure it is, but I'd risk it if that cop wasn't coming up behind us." He turned his signal on to get back on the road.

Joz let out the breath she'd been holding. "Dang, bad timing."

"Fucking too right." Turo smiled over at her, taking her hand in his. "However, every wolf in the club will know you're mine, so it's still a win."

She blinked, then groaned. "Oh my god, the scent thing, right?"

Turo squeezed his little mate's hand. She was damn sexy when she blushed. "Don't worry, they've seen, heard, and smelled it all, hahai."

By the time they reached the club, Turo had his raging erection back to almost semi-erect. He was coming to think Xan wasn't such a randy wolf as much as it was a normal state for a newly mated one. He may need to apologize for the times he'd accidentally on purpose interrupted the man and his mate. Or not. Yeah, probably not as it was too much fun to fuck with the young wolf whose mate called him Xander Mother-Fucking Carmichael. He was what they like to call, too extra. Although, in a fight or pinch, he was definitely the one Turo would call next to Kellen.

"There's an awful lot of cars here. I thought you guys had shut down the club or something?"

He looked around at all the unknown vehicles and tensed. "We'd already agreed to allow another club access for the night. I believe Kellen's vetted the group, so all's good. We'll not be here long. I need to talk to Kellen and let him know about our mated status, although he's probably already aware."

She raised her brows. "What do you mean?"

"He's the alpha. Anytime there's a new member added, through the alpha link, he feels it. I'm not exactly sure how it works, but since I've bonded with you, he should've felt that. Although since you haven't found your wolf yet, he might not. I don't know, but I want to formally tell him since we're here." Of course, he didn't like taking Jozlyn through the club with all the non-shifters and people he didn't know. The scent of a shifter he didn't recognize, but smelled like Kellen, caught his attention as soon as they entered.

The man stood up, he had dark hair and eyes that saw too much as he stepped in front of him and Jozlyn. The cut he wore proclaimed him part of the Iron Hammers, a club he'd heard of. Hell, he remembered Kellen and Xan had delivered a vehicle down into Texas just before Laikyn had delivered, coming back whooping about kicking ass and taking names.

"Names Joaquin," the wolf nodded at Turo. "Me and my boys came up to thank Kellen and Xan for their...help. Where's the little thing, Jenna? That chick...she's um, something else." He rocked back on his heels.

Turo looked the man over, wondering if his crew knew what they all were, if the wolf in front of him was planning on joining the Iron Wolves or if this was just a visit? "Have you talked to Kellen yet?"

"Yep! We're just having a few drinks before heading back out tomorrow. Great place you've got here." Joaquin nodded at the girls dancing up on the different raised platforms.

Joz snorted.

Joaquin's eyes landed on her. "And who might this gorgeous little thing be?"

"This is my mate," Turo announced with a warning none of the men could ignore.

The other wolf raised his hands. "That much was obvious, what with your bite and scent all over her. Congrats, man." Joaquin held his hand out. Turo glanced at it then did what felt right, took it in his, shaking it and accepting the man hug and back pounding.

"Names, Turo. This is my mate Jozlyn." He brought her to stand next to him.

With a slight tilt of his head, the other wolf turned and walked back to his table.

"Well, that was strange." Joz glanced up at Turo.

"I didn't give him permission to touch you. Come on, let's go see Kellen." He led her through the club and to the back where Kellen's office was. Before he could knock, his alpha's booming voice yelled for them to come in.

Inside, Kellen sat in his large leather recliner, a glass tumbler with amber liquid next to him. He stood as they entered. "Welcome to the pack, little sister." He held his arms open.

Joz froze. "Um, do I hug him?"

Kellen grinned. "Yes, but only briefly. I think Turo will try to rip my arms off if you linger, not to mention my mate and Team Styles are on their way. No need to have a strange female scent on me. My babes don't seem to care much for other scents just yet. Damn strange kiddos." His eyes shown with pride.

His mate walked the short distance and hugged Kellen then moved back to his side. "I haven't shifted yet."

"I know. There's something different about you, though. What's your heritage?" Kellen asked, sitting back down and picking up his drink, sipping slowly.

Joz tensed at his question. "My mother is Japanese and my father is American. Why?"

The alpha raised his brows over the rim. "Interesting. If Jenna were here, I'd have her do a looksee, but alas, I fear she's off getting herself mated to two wolpires," he sighed.

Turo tugged Joz further into the room and took a seat on the couch across from Kellen, pulling her onto his lap. "Have you heard from any of them?"

"No, the fuckers," Kellen growled. "I did reach out to Damikan, who has assured me Jenna is recovering. He'll make sure she gets in touch as soon as she's able, regardless of what his sons say. Lula has updated me on your two girls though." He pinned Joz and him with his alpha stare. "Asia and Egypt are well and wish to see you both once you're settled. I told Lula about your newly mated status and informed her you'd visit once Jozlyn has found her wolf. Lula of course said she'd help if you needed."

Turo's fingers contracted on her hip. "You did give a hard pass, right?"

Kellen grinned. "You scared of Lula?"

"Fuck yes," Turo agreed without missing a beat.

"Smart man."

Jozlyn raised her hand. "Who is Lula, and where did she take Egypt?"

"Ah, you still have a lot to learn. Baby girl, you need to take things in doses, small doses. Shift, find your wolf and then take that next step. Suffice it to say, your friends are in the safest place in the…universe."

Joz considered Kellen's words and then looked at the determination on his face. This man may be younger than her mate, but he was also the head honcho for a reason. She reached out to touch his mind, wondering if they had a link like Turo had said. Instant pain made her flinch.

"That's rude, little girl," Kellen admonished.

"She didn't know any better, and that was rude of you," Turo growled, coming to his feet and putting her behind him.

Turo and Kellen faced each other, both men almost equal in size and build. She hated being the cause of Turo and Kellen fighting, knowing her mate would give his life for hers. Kellen was clearly his boss, or alpha. Heck she was still learning the rules. "I'm sorry, I shouldn't have done that. Please forgive me," she pleaded, stepping between them.

"What the fuckity fuck is going on in here?" Laikyn asked, her voice no more than a whisper, but it had Kellen shifting away and closer to his mate.

"Mon chaton, why didn't you call me for help?"

Laikyn was pushing a stroller made for four into the room through the large door from the club's entrance.

"I did, you didn't answer me," she growled, glaring daggers at Kellen.

"Aw, shit. I put my walls up to keep that one out. She's got major mind skills." He moved to his mate, taking her into his arms.

Joz turned to look into Turo's eyes, mouthing *I'm sorry*.

"It's okay, hahai. What you did is normal. We tend to stretch our wings, or in your case new abilities. Kellen knows how it is." He looked at the alpha and his mate. A dare in his dark eyes.

Unease had her shivering. "I...I don't understand what I'm supposed to do, or feel, or how I'm supposed to act. Do you have a book or something? If one of you would just open up, I could sift through your thoughts and know the rules, but this minefield is hard. I don't like not knowing what to do." Never in her life had she been the one who didn't know the answers. Now, she had a great appreciation for her friends and classmates on test days, only this time it could be a matter of life and death.

Her mate, wrapped his large tattooed arms around her. "Hahai, I'll show you everything you need to know. My mind is an open door to you."

Without having to look at his face, she knew he was staring at Kellen in challenge. This wouldn't do. Turning, she brought her hands up to his cheeks. "Stop it. You can't be mad at him for doing what's natural to him. Imagine if anyone tried to do what I did. What would you have done? No, don't you dare say something that isn't the truth. You'd have done the same thing to him. Now, I'm going to go look at those adorable little nuggets while you and Kellen do that man hug thing."

Laikyn laughed. "Oh, she's an excellent addition to the pack."

"You only think that, 'cause she sassed me like all the rest of you women," Kellen grunted.

"She didn't sass you. She just exerted her alpha bitch," Laikyn pointed out.

Joz stopped and stared at Turo, seeing if he thought she was a bitch. "Alpha bitch is a good term, hahai." He winked.

"That had better be the only time I'm called a bitch by you, mate," she informed him.

Kellen clapped him on the back. "You need a drink." The alpha led him over to the bar in the corner.

For the first time since she and Turo connected, Joz wasn't sure he was happy until he looked over his shoulder. Heat and possibly the beginning of love lit his dark eyes.

"Come on, let's leave the testosterone menfolk here while I get a few things from the clinic. Kellen and Turo can watch the little angels while we run over there and back. With your help, I can get it done in one trip instead of two." Laikyn nodded like it was a foregone conclusion.

Kellen sat his glass down on the counter after swallowing the last of its contents. "Absolutely. I've got Turo here to help me. You good with changing dirty diapers?" he asked Turo.

A look of dismay crossed her mate's features. "Um, how about I go with Laikyn and Joz stay here?" he offered.

"That would be a hell no," Laikyn said, bending and kissing each of her babies before standing. "Come on, girl, let's go before they begin to cry like little beotches, and I don't mean my little angels."

Joz laughed at Kellen's growled warning of retribution. Turo crossed to her as she was about to be led out the door to the outside, the private exit reserved for Kellen. He stopped Laikyn from flinging the door open, his body blocking their exit. "Slow down, woman." His big body leaned out, then he sniffed. "All's clear. Be sure you check for danger before you walk outside, Laikyn. Joz's wolf hasn't come out yet, so her sense of smell isn't as good as yours."

"Yes, sir," Laikyn agreed smartly.

Chapter Fifteen

"It's harder than fuck to watch them leave, ain't it?" Kellen moved the stroller closer to his chair, watching his children sleep could become his next favorite thing to do.

"Like ripping my heart out and laying it on the ground to be stomped on," he agreed.

Kellen chuckled. "That's a pretty accurate way to describe it, but look at these little angels." He waved his hand at the stroller. "Wait till you have a baby of your own then you'll realize just how much more your world becomes a danger zone."

"Your babies are like a couple days old." Turo looked at the sleeping babes, thinking they were probably the cutest kids he'd seen. Of course, when he and Joz had one of their own, he was sure theirs would be just as cute, if not cuter, but he'd keep that bit to himself.

"Fuck, I knew it the moment I realized these guys were in Laikyn's stomach. If I could've created a bubble strong enough to enclose her and our children, I'd have done it. Hell, I asked Jenna to do just that, but that crazy Fey only laughed at me. Bestie my ass," he growled, making the two boys stir, their blue eyes blinking open. Kellen quickly began moving the stroller back and forth in a soothing manner.

"Well, I for one am all for working on the Fey Queen to make one for our mates."

The alpha held his hand up for a high five as both of his sons closed their eyes again. Turo tapped Kellen's hand lightly, not wanting to make too much noise. Although he didn't think the children would wake up, he wasn't risking it. Nope, he wasn't going to be changing diapers and having them throw up on him if he could avoid it.

The clock on the wall ticked as another five minutes passed. He and Kellen sipped on their drinks, neither of them saying much. After fifteen minutes had passed, he stood. "What's taking so long?"

Kellen shrugged. "Laikyn ordered some special milk since she's not producing enough to feed all four of these guys."

Turo raised his brows. "I bet." The two boys looked like they were gonna be brawlers like their dad, while the girls truly did look like little angels.

"Don't let appearances fool you. I'm betting these two will be the ones who give me grey hair first." He ran a finger down one of the girls' cheeks then the other ones.

"You think you can handle them on your own? I'm gonna go check on our mates." Turo paced to the door, his hand on the thick steel, willing Kellen to give an affirmative answer.

A tip of his dark head was enough to have him moving through the door, making sure it locked solidly behind him. His wolf was clawing at his insides. Opening his link to Joz, he tried to get in touch, needed to know she was okay. Her walls blocked him, making both he and his wolf snarl. "We are gonna knock that shit right the fuck down when I see you, hahai," he promised. His long legs ate up the distance from Kellen's private entrance and around to the back lot of the parking area. He scanned the parked cars, looking for what he didn't know, only knew something was out of place. His eyes landed on Coti and Laikyn. His friend's arms held several bags, but his mate was nowhere to be seen.

"Where's Joz?" he asked as they reached him.

"Oh, she told me she was going to tell you. She went home to get a few changes of clothes and some…whoa, Turo, didn't she tell you?" Laikyn called after him.

His mind roared at the ignorance of his mate. The whole too stupid to live thing popped into his head. What the hell was she thinking? Fuck, she was putting a huge target on her head. The thought had him pausing as he grabbed the handle to his truck. "Laikyn, was she alone at all at the clinic? Did you notice something off about her or anything?"

The alpha's mate chewed on her bottom lip. "I don't know. Maybe. I mean she sort of froze on me before we entered the door, like something had grabbed ahold of her or...I don't know. It was weird, but she laughed it off. It wasn't until a few minutes after we were inside she looked at her clothes and exclaimed she really needed her own things. I...holy shit, do you think someone made her leave?"

Coti grabbed Laikyn around the waist and began hauling her toward the club. "Go. I'll make sure she's with Kellen, and then I'm right behind you."

Turo didn't answer. His mate could even now be in the hands of the vampire hybrid who would use her for his own twisted needs. "Son-of-a-bitch. Why'd I let you go alone?" He gunned the engine of his big truck, barely giving the men at the gates a glance as he skidded out of the lot. His mate's mind was normally closed, but that was only because he didn't use the force he could. With her life on the line, Turo didn't worry about pissing off the one who held his heart. Hundreds of years of forming his entire being into a weapon much stronger than even his beloved guns, he barreled through with ease. The first thing he found was chaos. Joz was fighting against the onslaught of the monster trying to control her, and she was losing. "Keep fighting, hahai. I'm coming for you. Open your eyes and show me where you are."

Dammit, he needed her to give him some direction. If he went on Laikyn's timeframe, Joz had a fifteen-minute head start on him. His truck's Hemi engine would hopefully make up half that time if not more. Goddess, he prayed like he'd never done before he was able to save her, or he wouldn't survive either.

Jozlyn felt a disturbance in the air. Her immediate response was to throw up mental blocks, but she felt the same chill she had back at the hospital, the same one that Egypt's monster of a father gave off. Her first priority was keeping her new family and friends' safe. Laikyn may be a shifter, but she was a mother with four babies to care for. If Joz could lead the bastard away from where those precious children were, then he'd have to follow her. The reason he was there wasn't for them but her. She knew his type, and his thirst for revenge would be deep. Oh yes, she could write a book on the workings of a psychopath such as Kenneth, even though he was clearly not a simple human.

It took a little convincing to get Laikyn to understand her need for clothing. Of course, she also told the other woman she would be reaching out to Turo as well...a small lie, one that she hoped Laikyn couldn't sense.

"Turo is going to follow me. Oh, don't forget you can't spoil your babies by holding them too much." Joz began spouting off the facts about spoiling children and the facts that were found to back up the findings. Her friend's eyes did the slight glazed look most did, when she began reciting numbers and long drawn out explanations. She'd done the same to teachers in school, only she hadn't recognized the signs of boredom at the time.

"Alright, go on then. I'll make my way back. I believe I have a shadow anyhow." Laikyn pointed over her shoulder.

The large man named Coti lifted a shoulder but didn't appear apologetic. "Hey, I'm following orders. Besides, it's better than being in the club and watching a bunch of asshats try to dance."

Joz left the two of them, as they began going through supplies. Before she opened the thick door, she took a deep breath. "Alright wolf girl, if you're in there, now would be a really good time to push to the front and be ready to help me."

She felt a stirring inside her, a foreign yet familiar presence. The entity didn't quite seem like a wolf, not like what she'd seen in Turo's memories, but she accepted the being as hers. Outside, she lifted her head and scented the air, much like she'd seen Turo do. On the wind, she caught the faintest hint of old rotting vegetation, enough she knew Kenneth was near. Hurrying to her car, she unlocked it, wishing for the umpteenth time it had auto-unlocks.

"Come get me you bastard," she whispered once she turned out of the lot. A glance at her fuel level told her she'd be fine for the short distance to her house, which sat on the opposite side of town to where Turo's was. "Why did I choose a house in the woods instead of one in a nice housing development?" She shifted to third gear as she rounded a curve, screaming as a man stood in her path. She jerked the wheel to the right, her foot jammed on the brake as she barreled through the guardrail. Trees lined the side of the road, and luckily for her, the incline wasn't steep, nor was there a drop off. However, by the time she came to a stop thanks to a large Pine, her little VW took a lot of damage to the hood and her windshield was cracked.

It took her moments to unbuckle and pry her door open. Moments that seemed like an eternity as she felt like she was being hunted. Wetness trickled down her face, making her curse as she wiped it away and saw the red stain on her fingers. "Great, exactly what I need. I should just lie down here and wait for the asshats to find me." Reaching into her car, she pulled out Egypt's hospital gown and used it to wipe her own blood on. Then, realizing the monster chasing her would be tracing both scents, she did her best to staunch the cut on her forehead with the cloth, then she gathered up her wits and began running along the highway back to the club. If he'd been on the road, Kenneth would already be on her. He was clearly using up energy to scare her, probably trying to lure her to where he wants her to go. Well, her first instinct was to run farther into the woods. Now, she took to the road near the highway. If a car happened by, then she'd flag it down. She wasn't one of those too stupid to live heroines in books and never would be. Where did that thought come from?

A sedan was coming around the corner. She waved her arms over her head, hoping it would stop. The tinted windows of the luxury vehicle didn't lower. Joz realized her mistake the moment the back door opened and Kenneth stepped out. "Hello Dr. Rasey. What a pleasant surprise, me finding you on the side of the road. Did you have an...accident?"

She backed away, but had only taken a step before he gripped her arm and flung her inside the dark car. "Move it before the wolf bastards come for their bitch."

Joz had a moment of panic and then calmness stole over her. "What do you want?"

"I want back what's mine. I think once I have you nice and...in pain, you'll tell me where my property is, or I'll bleed you until you're useless to me then your wolf will come, and I'll get answers from him."

Joz tried to sit up, pushing her hair out of her face. The small cut on her head began to bleed again, causing the monster in the vehicle to snarl. "You're wrong. Turo won't come for me, and none of the others will either. Your property," she paused to wipe her sweaty hands on her pants, watching the bastard's eyes track her movements. "Egypt and her mother are far away from here, in a location I don't know about. The wolf as you call him, didn't tell me where. So you see, you've wasted precious time and energy in this." She waved her hand around the interior of the car.

He sat back with a smirk. "Ah, you're wrong, you little bitch."

She wanted to smack him for his words but held the urge in check. "How is that?"

Kenneth's arm came toward her before she was aware he'd moved, pulling her close to him. The scent of blood and death hung over him like a cloak. "Because you're his mate. A wolf would never allow his mate to be taken. You see, once a wolf mates, it's for life. By me taking you, your mate will hunt me to the ends of the earth to find you, sacrifice his own life for yours. Only he doesn't realize your life has already been wasted."

Joz screamed as sharp yellow teeth burst from Kenneth's mouth. Unlike when she'd seen Turo shift, this beast truly was a monster. His words became garbled, and his gums were blackened.

Her wolf, or whatever, which had been just out of reach, roared inside her. She'd always been a fighter, had trained in many martial art forms since she'd been a child. Even at close range, her one-inch punch could put most men on their backs. Strength flowed through her, more than any she'd ever expected to feel, an infusion the likes of which she would have feared had it not been a matter of life and death. As she punched Kenneth in the face with the move that had made Bruce Lee famous, his howl of anger made the man driving the car swerve dangerously close to the edge. She caught a glimpse of the driver in the mirror staring back at her. Human, but if she had to guess, Kenneth controlled the man's mind, probably fed off him too.

Kenneth released her as blood poured from his shattered nose. Using his distraction, she tried to jerk the door open, cursing when the thing wouldn't budge. "God damn locks."

She pulled the lever up and then tossed her body out of the moving vehicle. At thirty miles an hour, she expected a few bumps and bruises, but dang, her hands and knees hit the pavement hard. The screech of tires had her getting up from the ground where she'd finally stopped rolling, feeling as if she'd been hit by a truck. The need to move had her pushing up onto her hands and knees then onto her feet. She swayed a bit, until finally the world stopped spinning. The vehicle was coming back toward her at an alarming rate. Taking a deep breath, she hit the woods and ran full out, opening her mind to Turo as she felt him batter her mind.

"I'm coming hahai, stay alive no matter what," he ordered.

Bossy wolf. *"That's high on my priorities."*

"Keep this link open no matter what. I don't want to have to fight your blocks, baby."

Her heart stuttered then restarted. *"I know it's really soon, and we don't know each other, but I think I could love you. If something happens, I just wanted you to know that."*

"Don't fucking talk like I'm not gonna get there in time. And, when I do, you and I are gonna have a long ass discussion about boundaries and feelings. I've waited hundreds of years for my mate. I'm not

letting you go now. You're mine. My mate, my love, my everything, hahai."

The fine hairs on the back of her neck stood on end as she pumped her arms and legs trying to get as far away from the road as possible. She looked back to see if anyone was behind her, when a hard object stopped her in her tracks. All the air left her lungs as she landed on her ass. Looking up she saw not Kenneth the man but Kenneth the monster. He'd dropped the façade of humanity, taking on the appearance of his vampire/shifter form, only he wasn't anything like what she'd seen Turo as a wolf look like. No, he looked like a reject from a chemical plant explosion with fangs and hair. "Oh my gawd, you really should have someone look at that." She scooted backward in a crab-like walk.

Kenneth growled. "If you wouldn't have taken my girl and that bastard wolf taken my mate, I wouldn't be like this. I need them," he growled.

Saliva dripped from his fangs, and he walked on half human, half panther legs. His body had grown to almost double his size. Shit, she was so screwed.

"I don't know what to tell you. I don't have them, and as you can see, no wolves are coming to rescue me." She stalled for time, feeling Turo was close.

When Kenneth growled, his head raised to the sky. She used the distraction to get to her feet. With the intent to run, she tried to figure out the best direction to go, but then, his laugh had her looking back toward him. "You think you can escape me?" He took one disfigured step in her direction than another.

Joz took a step back for each one he took forward, like a chess game, only she was losing ground since his legs were longer. Finally, Joz concluded her wolf wasn't going to come out anytime soon, or she'd have by now. That incessant itching was still there, but no hair sprouted. What she hadn't realized was the beast had been corralling her into a corner until her back hit a dirt wall. Panicking, she looked left and right.

Fine, he wanted to kill her, she'd make sure he choked or at least hurt a little. Years of training had her bowing to him like he was an opponent. "Come on you ugly bastard." She waved him toward her then didn't say anything as she felt an inner stirring that was more...powerful. Her vision became clearer as did her hearing. This time when he charged her, she struck out with her leg, knocking him on his ass. His growl of anger had the leaves around them shaking, making her think of the saying *'shaking like a leaf'* only she wasn't shaking. No, whatever had woken inside her was ready to emerge.

Joz spun and kicked, her arms and legs moving faster than she'd ever done as she launched herself at Kenneth. Their battle would've been epic and over quickly had the sun not dropped and revealed he had backup. She felt him calling his friends and could do nothing except reach out and break his neck. The snap had her gagging, but he was far from salvageable. How she knew what to do, or how to do it, she wasn't sure. There was a part of her being that was taking over while she seemed to be a watcher, taking it all in.

The scent of Turo hit her, thanks to her newfound abilities. "Holy fuck, Hahai." Turo glanced at the twitching body on the ground. "We need to take his heart out."

At his words, she did gag a little. "Not sure I can do that."

Turo ran his hand over her head then pulled her into his body, hugging her tightly. "I'll do it."

Joz hated her weakness, but then a girl could be forgiven when she'd just killed a monster. Right?

Her mate bent, keeping one foot on the ground the other he placed on top of Kenneth's head. He then turned to Joz. "Look away," he ordered.

The sound of bones crushing and a sucking wetness was almost more than she could handle. Holy shit, she'd gone to med school and never lost her lunch at any of the clinics she'd done, yet here she was ready to toss it over seeing…okay, so hearing your guy rip another being's heart out was definitely out of the norm.

"I need to destroy this. Fire would be best, but I don't have a lighter on me."

She looked at Turo's naked body then instinct had her moving toward him. "I can do it."

Turo raised a brow.

Joz wasn't sure what had her holding her hand out, but that inner being was taking over again. Turo gave her the blackened heart and then she opened her mouth and took a deep breath. When she blew out again, fire erupted, setting the organ on fire. She dropped the heart on the ground, shaking her hand but quickly realized she wasn't burned.

Turo stomped on the ground, making sure they didn't set the forest on fire. Once the heart was destroyed, Kenneth's body disintegrated. "Fuck me running, Joz."

"I don't even know what to say," she whispered looking at the ground.

He opened his mouth to respond then paused, sniffing the air. "Shit, I hope you got more of that inside you, 'cause we've got company."

She stiffened as her nose caught the smell of rotting flesh. "How many?"

"I think four, maybe five." Turo gripped the back of her hair and brought her face back. "When we get out of this, I'm gonna fuck you so damn hard you ain't gonna be walking, much less running for a few days, feel me?"

Joz licked her lips. "Promise?"

"Oh yeah. I don't break promises. Now, find that inner fire breathing whatever and tell her she's gotta come out and play."

"I think she's a dragon. I felt scales ripple over my skin for a second."

Chapter Sixteen

Turo stared at his mate and had to blink twice before he could get his tongue to work. He'd met a man in a small village in Japan hundreds of years ago. The old man had told him one day he'd meet his match with a dragon lady. Turo had thought he meant in the sense she'd be...a bitch or some shit. Now, he wondered if the man had seen the future. However, his musings were cut short as the two vampires came into the small space Kenneth had lured his mate into.

"We don't have an issue with you boys. I suggest you turn and go back to where you came from." Turo placed himself in front of Joz, drawing the men's gazes.

One of the men grinned showing his vampire teeth were dropped down, ready to bite. "Well, that's where you're wrong shifter. You see, we know what happens when a vampire drinks from a shifter. We would get to walk in the sun again. Our strength would increase, and we wouldn't keep rotting away like yesterday's trash. So, yeah, you do have an issue with us. If you were smart you'd just hand us the female, and we'll let you live."

He took a deep breath, then waved his hand in front of his face. "Now, that's a shame," Turo said not bothering to address anything they said.

The other vampire nudged his friend. "What is a shame?"

"Well as I see it, you had all these great ideas and plans, but it's a shame 'cause you could've just went on about your business if you'd done as I said. Hence, that's a shame." Turo shifted before either man could decide what was going on. His wolven jaws tore out the throat of one of the vampires, twisting in the air to rake his claws against the other's back. He raced back toward Joz, coming up short as he saw she'd ripped out the one vampire's heart and set it on fire.

In his wolf form, he circled the other vampire, the scent of burning flesh assaulted his sensitive nose. Goddess, he hated the smell of burning vampire, which he didn't know until just this moment. He reached out to Joz, wanting to make sure she was okay. Her calmness settled him, and his task of taking down the newly made vamp.

Turo was sure they'd dispatch the being, and he could make good on his promise in no time flat. Of course, that was before the smell of two more of the fiends hit him. "*Joz, two more are coming.*" He wondered where the fifth was, 'cause as sure as the sun sets in the west, he was sure there was a fifth.

If his mate wasn't here, he'd not be worried, but her dragon, or whatever she thought she was hadn't emerged. Hell, he didn't think there were dragons on earth and wondered if her wolf was rebelling at whatever was inside her.

He fell to his side, sharp pain assaulting his back as one of the newcomers hit him with a downed tree. Fuck, how strong were these fuckers? He rolled over, leaves and dirt kicking up as he tried to regain purchase. The third vampire moved in, helping the others form a half circle, leaving Joz behind them. Clearly, they didn't see her as a threat. Good!

"*Xan and Bodhi are on their way with my cousin Joaquin, jackass. Next time don't leave without backup.*" Kellen's voice was low and deadly.

He wasn't going to apologize or explain to his alpha since the other man could read his thoughts. His back was on fire from whatever had hit him, and his mate was behind a wall of bloodsuckers. Yeah, he wasn't too proud or stupid to take help.

"Look at the dog. Where's the leash?" One of the vampires snapped his fingers.

Turo's eyes narrowed on the bastard. A growl of fury built in his lungs, boiling out and then he lunged, dropping low at the last second. He'd seen the calculation in the being's eyes. He'd been taunting Turo, but what he didn't know was Turo was a master manipulator. Instead of going for his throat, he slashed at his stomach, deep and hard, spilling the man's insides out. Oh yeah, he may not die right away, can probably regenerate, but he was out of the fight.

"Turo, did you just gut that man?" Joz questioned.

His mate's voice entered his mind. *"If I say yes, will you gag again?"*

Joz sniffed and flipped him off in his mind, the image had him smiling, the action in wolf form probably not nearly as normal looking. He wasn't focused on the two vamps, therefore unprepared for them to tag team him. Hell, he was going to get his ass chewed by Kellen if he found out.

"Looks like we're just in time to save his big ass," Xan said with his arms hanging at his side.

He and Bodhi shifted on the fly and then they were ripping into the vampires as the other man who resembled Kellen turned to face the woods. Another vampire they hadn't seen landed in front of the wolf. He fought like their alpha, fast and deadly, taking the vamps head off without pausing to say a word.

Turo rolled out of the way as he saw Bodhi going for the throat of the one closest to him, allowing his friend the killing bite. He lay on his back panting, knowing his mate was standing by waiting to burn the hearts.

"Sheot, anybody bring a lighter to the party?" Bodhi asked, his body showing a few bloody claw marks.

"Goodness, do all of you just walk around naked as the day you were born?" Joz asked as she walked up, rubbing her hands together.

"Don't look below their shoulders, hahai," Turo groaned, shifting on the ground to a sitting position.

"He doesn't want you to realize we're all much larger than him." Xan held his hands a couple feet apart. The action making Bodhi laugh and give Xan a high five.

"You realize the man you just high fived is fucking your baby sister's best friend, the girl you treat as your own, right?" Turo got to his feet, raising his brows as Xan realized what that meant.

"Fuck you, T, that was rude." Xan glared at him. "Here we rushed to save your big ass and everything."

Bodhi laughed. "Dude, how about we worry about what we're gonna do about these fuckers. I guess we could take their hearts with us." He shuddered.

"I'm just here to lend a helping hand, not get into a convo about dick size, but if," he stopped as Turo moved in front of him. "Whoa, she's your old lady. I got enough problems on my hands, don't need another. How the fuck we get rid of these fuckers?" Joaquin pointed at the dead men, tossing the head he had in his hand into the pile and drug the body over with the others.

"Take his heart out," Turo instructed.

The other man's eyes narrowed, but he punched his fist through the chest cavity and then tossed the organ in the air.

Jozlyn walked forward. "Um, I got this. Lay them down there."

Bodhi and Xan tossed the hearts into a pile followed by Joaquin, and before their eyes, his mate did a little huff and puff, and then she burnt the hearts away.

"Dayum, she's like the wolf in the stories, only she's not blowing the house down." Xan stood with his hands on his hips.

Turo took a deep breath. "That's why his mate calls him Xander Mother-Fucking Carmichael. One just can't help it when dealing with him. Shift fuckers, and let's go back to the club. I wish Jenna were here so she could help us with figuring out what's going on with my mate." Turo pulled Joz against him, kissing her on the mouth.

Xan raised his middle finger up, and then he blew on it, raising his hand higher. "Blow on this," Xan said then shifted.

"You gotta love him though. I mean, he gets shit done and makes no apologies on how he does it." Bodhi pointed at the vampire Xan had taken out, the arms and legs had been ripped off and placed back with the arms in place of the legs and vice versa. "He drove so better go. See you both at the club. We'll figure you out or not. Whatever you are, little sister, you're one of us." Bodhi nodded then shifted.

Joaquin tilted his head then shifted, too, racing after the other men.

Joz blinked up at Turo. "Why haven't they gone poof like the other one?"

"Can you burn the bodies." He glared at the vampires. "Maybe 'cause they're still newish?" Turo wasn't sure why they hadn't gone to dust yet, only knew they couldn't leave them there for humans to find. As Joz opened her mouth to breathe, the bodies began to disintegrate, saving her from the job.

Chapter Seventeen

Kellen sat in his chair with Laikyn in his lap, the children were asleep and being watched by Lyric and Syn with their mates. He looked at the newest addition to the pack and scratched his jaw. She had always had a different scent to him, but he'd assumed it was due to her encounter with the cat shifters. Now, he inhaled deeply, smelling Turo's wolf on her along with her own. Oh yes, she was a wolf, but she had Fey in her. More than they had with the others.

"Your mother's family is from Japan?" he questioned her.

Jozlyn nodded. "Yes. My great great grandmother came here with her husband, much to her family's dismay. Why?"

"I wonder if you aren't one of the few in the Goddess touched lineage. It would explain your ability to do things the rest of us can't. You have a wolf in you. I can help you change now if you'd like. I know your mate wants you to let it come naturally, but I think your natural abilities are blocking your wolf." He held his hand up as Turo opened his mouth. "I know you're far older than I am, Arturo. I respect you as an elder, but I'm the alpha. I'll also respect you as her mate, but trust me on this."

Turo breathed deeply. "Joz, it's up to you. However, I agree with Kellen. I think you have such complete control of your mind, your wolf may never fully emerge if not forced. I can't do it. My wolf won't allow me to, but Kellen can."

Joz squeezed Turo's hand. "Okay. When?"

Kellen patted his mate's thigh, their eyes meeting, and he stood. "Now."

He watched the little female's eyes widen, felt his pack mate's need to protect his own female. "Xan, I'm going to need you and Coti to hold Turo back. His wolf is ready to rip through right now, but I have a feeling as soon as this little thing's wolf is free, he's going to be a happy wolf."

"Fuck that, Kellen. I don't think it's wise to force her, if you think it's going to make me wild."

"Anything that's out of your control will do that, Turo. Now, sit in here until I call you out. Five minutes tops. Laikyn will come with me. Know that I'd never harm your mate, especially with my own so close."

Kellen allowed his alpha powers to wash over the men and women in his office. Xan nodded yet didn't show him his throat. Coti turned his head, giving him a clear view of his. One by one, the wolves who were his pack, except for the more dominant like Xan and Turo, who glared at him showed their throats. "See, that's why I need them to hold you. I won't harm a hair on her head. You've my solemn vow, Arturo." His word was law, and a vow was as good as a law. Unbreakable.

Turo nodded. "You good with this, Joz?"

Jozlyn licked her lips then stood on her tiptoes and kissed Turo. When they pulled away, Kellen knew they'd spoken through their link.

"Let's get this done, so I can have some private time with my mate."

Xan cleared his throat. "Isn't it too soon for you two…to you know, get it on?"

Kellen flipped him off then walked outside with Laikyn laughing. Joz followed, but he knew she was scared. He could feel her emotions. Yes, they were all Fey to an extent, but he sensed more in her. If Jenna were here, he was sure she'd be able to tell him exactly what, but once her wolf came out, he'd know. They'd all know. Either way, she needed to be whole.

Taking a deep breath, he closed his eyes then opened them when he felt Turo's presence entering the clearing behind the club. He'd known the other wolf wouldn't be able to allow his mate out of his sight.

Turo took Jozlyn's hand. "We do this together."

"As it should be. Now, we do this and then we drink, or you two do whatever." Kellen waved his hand. Laikyn stepped back.

He kissed Joz's forehead. "Focus on Kellen, and do what he says. He'd never do anything to hurt you. I'm here. I'll always be here."

She bit her lip. "I know. Let's do this."

Kellen growled, the low rumble of his alpha wolf vibrated through the woods. The hair on Turo's body stood on end as he felt his alpha connect with Joz. Her mind opened to him, sharing what was going on. Intelligent blue eyes shone brightly in the darkness. Turo was shocked at the imagery, and then he watched as the blue eyes formed into Kellen's large wolf form. Turo hung back as the wolf stalked through the darkness until a light lit up showing the form of a dragon. Kellen walked up to the dragon and touched noses with it. Conversation seemed to flow between the two beings, and then the dragon lifted dark eyes. His mate's eyes stared out at him from the dragon.

Turo held his breath, waiting to see what would happen, if the dragon would move out of the darkness, and if that was his mate's other form. Hell, he wasn't sure how they'd let her stretch her wings, but they'd do it. As he watched and waited, the gorgeous dragon shifted to a black wolf. She was about a third the size of Kellen's, but she didn't shy away from the alpha as he butted his head against hers. His wolf growled, and then sat on its haunches as his mate turned her head. Love shone out at him.

The scent of earth hit him, making him acutely aware of being brought out of Joz's mind.

"Wow and they called me a pussy for…um falling at the birth of my kids." Kellen squatted next to him.

Shaking his head, Turo tried to make sense of what he was saying. "What the hell are you talking about?" He stood up and dusted the dirt off his ass then stopped as he noticed the small black wolf. "Holy fucking shit. You shifted. Fuck, she's a black wolf. She's…" he was at a loss for words.

Laikyn patted him on the arm. "It's okay, we won't tell anyone you passed out and yes, your mate is a gorgeous black wolf. Now, I'm taking my mate back to check on our babies. You two go do what new mates do. Well, not in the woods, 'cause ew." Laikyn shuddered.

Kellen pulled his mate into his arms. "You didn't say that when I..." Laikyn covered his mouth, keeping him from finishing.

Turo walked over to Jozlyn. He got down on his knees and held his arms out. "You're beautiful no matter what form hahai."

The little wolf shifted on her paws then charged him. He caught her and rolled, as she hit him in the chest. Goddess, he was a lucky fucking bastard. Hundreds of years and he'd thought he'd missed his mate somewhere along the line or wasn't good enough to have one. Now, he'd found her, and she was perfect. Fate may be fickle, but she wasn't always a bitch.

Jozlyn nipped his chin. "You want to run?" The black wolf shifted away. "Open your mind and our link will weave together and solidify, hahai."

He held his breath and prayed it would. Goddess, he prayed. All the other males had talked about the miracle of instantaneous togetherness they felt. Although he already felt connected to Joz unlike any other, he wanted that bond.

As soon as her mind opened to his, he heard a buzzing sound and then wind whipped around him like a tsunami. His first instinct was to grab Jozlyn, pulling her wolven body into his arms.

The form of the old Japanese man from long ago appeared. "Ah, Arturo, I see you have found your dragon lady. Very good. Now, you and she are one. I've waited many years to see you again." He bowed at the waist. "You're a stubborn wolf. It took a stubborn female to be your mate. Alas, my great great great granddaughter fills those shoes. My wife Kiyoki thought I was crazy when I'd told her about the wolf man who would one day marry into our family. Now, I can go and tell her I was right."

Jozlyn shifted back, wearing the same clothes she'd had on. "Who are you?"

The old man moved forward, touching her forehead. Images flashed into her mind and Turo's. He saw his past and how it had collided with Haruaki. At the time, the old man had fallen and had almost been run over by a horse. Turo had saved him without thought, which then had the man inviting him to eat with his family.

"I see you remember. Yes, you saved my life, and I told you I would save yours. Now, that debt is paid." Haruaki bowed again. "Gukou yama o utsusu," the older man said, the old proverb of faith can move mountains, hitting him like a punch. He'd climbed mountain after mountain to find his mate. Hell, he'd move mountains for his fated mate.

"Thank you, great grandfather. I promise to keep him safe from here on out." Jozlyn slipped her arm around Turo's waist; a tremor swept over her tiny frame.

"I think it is I who needs to work harder at keeping you safe," Turo looked down at his female, shocked at the green ring circling her dark eyes.

"She has the heart of a dragon in her." Haruaki answered his unspoken question. "I must go now. Take care of each other."

The wind whipped up, leaving them alone in the clearing.

"I don't know about you, but that was strange as heck," Joz said glancing at the spot where her grandfather had been.

Turo laughed. "You know, I just realized you don't curse much, or at least not that I've noticed."

Joz turned in the circle of his arms, looping her arms around his neck. "Hmm, well, you do it enough for the both of us. Holy shit, my car," she gasped.

"Reeves already went to get it and will have her fixed back to its pristine condition in no time. Wanna go for a run in your wolf form?" Turo asked.

His mate sighed, snuggling against him. "Can we go by my place and get a few things then go back to yours? I'm sort of whipped. Plus, I still need to find out if I'm fired and figure out what I'm going to tell my parents."

He turned them back toward the parking lot, coming to a stop at the pink haired bombshell standing in the middle of the lot with her hands on her hips. She gave them a little wave then headed their way. "Just the two I was looking for. Whew, do you have any clue how taxing it is fixing human minds? Oh, sorry, you sorta do that for a living. Don't worry, I didn't fix all the humans so you'd be outta job or anything. Actually, that's what I came to tell you."

"Um, Lula, can you explain that a little better? You know for the slower class." Turo gripped Joz closer as she froze next to him.

"Oh, I should introduce myself." Lula slapped her hand on her forehead. "I forget to do those things sometimes. "Hiya, I'm LulaBell, but you can call me Lula. Um, I'm from the Fey Realm, and I fixed your job prob. So, yeah. What else did you want me to tell you?" She blinked sparkling violet eyes with a green ring circling them up at Turo.

Turo looked at Joz and noticed she had that same green color ringing her eyes. Lula was a dragon of sorts. He wondered if she could sense the being in Joz but didn't want to call attention to his mate any more than what was already on her. Heck, Joz looked like she was on the verge of crying.

Joz held up her palm. "Okay, let me get this straight. You did something at the hospital to make it what? Okay about Egypt being gone? What about the…death of Tilly?

Lula placed her finger over her mouth and tapped. "Well, I made it to where Egypt was never there. It's easier to scrub away than fudge records. As for Tilly, who BTW was a nasty woman, rest her soul with Hades, she died from a terrible fall down the steps. Bam. I also made it to where you've been on vaca," Lula paused and pumped her arms up and down. "What. Who's your girl Friday now?" Lula dusted her knuckles on her black tank top, which had an image of Deadpool riding a unicorn.

"How did you explain the huge gaping wound in her abdomen and my patients who saw a monster?" Oh god, she forgot all about Aleria.

"Human minds are not all that complex. No offense. I just floated through the hospital, fixing and…bam. Oh, and Aleria is fixed too. That child really had it rough. Although, she was already on the right path, from what you'd told her to do.

However, what she saw kinda messed with her. I fixed her 'cause I liked her aura. I think she'll be alright now. Her aunt is a nice woman. I made sure before I left her with the woman. I'll do a looksee every once in a while, to check in on her. Anyhoo, while Jennaveve is recovering, I thought I'd take care of her people." She leaned in close and whispered. "BTW, you're her people."

Joz let go of Turo and wrapped her arms around Lula. "Thank you so much."

Lula stiffened then hugged her back. "You're my sisterkin. How did that happen? Where've you been?" She pulled back and looked Joz up and down.

Turo put his hands on Joz's shoulders. "We're not sure exactly, only that she has a fierce wolf with a little dragon inside her."

"This is awesome," Lula cried. "Do you have a tattoo? Let me see," she said with a tinge of excitement and tried to lift Jozlyn's shirt.

"What the heck are you talking about?" Jozlyn stepped away from Lula then looked down at her hip as her drawstring on her pants had come undone. "Turo?"

He lifted the hem of her shirt. They both gasped at the image of a red and green dragon, covering her hip and down her thigh. The head flaring up her back while the tail wrapped around her leg. "I guess I got a tattoo."

Lula clapped her hands. "She's gorgeous." Lula turned and showed them her back. The pink and green dragon took up most of her back. It's piercing green eyes looked almost as if they were watching them. "I need to go back home. Take care of her, and she'll take care of you." Lula kissed Joz's cheek then Turo's.

"Tell Egypt and Asia…I don't know, that I said hi and that they don't need to worry anymore." Joz looked at Turo who nodded.

Lula saluted them. "If I'd have been there, I'd have eaten him. No, he'd have probably tasted like roadass." She gagged.

"You mean roadkill?" Joz asked.

The woman shrugged. "Same diff. Gotta go. Toodles." She gave a wave and then she disappeared.

"Where did she go? Oh god, I think I'm gonna faint." Joz held onto him as he lifted her into his arms.

He laughed. "You burn bad guys to a crisp, turn into a wolf, talk to your great grandfather like ten times removed, yet you get faint over her popping out? Come on woman, let's get you some clothes and head home."

She snuggled. "Sounds about right."

Joz woke to find herself wrapped in the warm embrace of her mate. She was still finding it hard to wrap her head around everything that'd happened. She inhaled, loving his smells. Lord, she hadn't really noticed other men had unique scents, other than whatever cologne they wore. However, Turo smelled divine.

"I've been waiting for you to wake up," his voice rumbled.

She looked up, seeing he was wide awake. "How long you been up?"

He looked at the clock. "About an hour. You're cute when you snore."

Joz was mortified. then she saw the glimmer of amusement in his stare. She pinched his side, or tried. "No fair. You have no fat. Look," her fingers tried gripping him again, slipping off to snap instead. "How is that even fair?"

"I have something else you can wrap your fingers around," he said.

She blinked up at him, sleep clouding her brain. After they'd gotten enough clothes, the charger for her phone, along with her laptop and bathroom supplies, she was wiped out. She didn't even remember the ride back to his place. Now, she let his words sink in and grinned.

"Oh really? Would you like me to pinch your fatty?" She trailed her hand down his stomach,

He grinned. "Well, pinching wouldn't be my first option, but your fingers wrapping around him sure sounds nice." Then his eyes widened. "Wait, we don't call him fatty."

Joz tried to wrap her fingers around his hardness, but she couldn't quite encircle him. "Hey, I'm just going along with what you called it."

His hand covered hers, showing her the motion he liked. "No, I just suggested something else you could…" he moaned as her thumb swiped over the tip. "Damn, what was I saying?"

"I've no clue," she said looking down at her hand and his. When she went to move her head down, wanting to taste him, he stopped her.

"I want to taste you, too." His grin was positively wicked. "Sixty-nine is truly the best number."

She squeezed the head of his dick. "Oh really?"

He grunted, putting his hand over hers. "Anyone before you are nothing but a memory. You are my everything. You're my present, my gift, my future. My reason for living."

"See, you go and say the sweetest things and make me all weepy." Joz kissed his chest.

"I hope you're weepy down south, 'cause you're also the sweetest pussy in all the universes, and I'm a starving man. Sit on my face, woman."

Jozlyn laughed, then groaned as he lifted her, positioning her legs on either side of his face as if she weighed nothing. "You really are a dirty man, Arturo. And, I love it," she moaned, leaning forward to grip his cock in her hand.

As he used his hands to spread her pussy lips open for him teasing and licking, taking her up to heights of pleasure that had her screaming his name, she used her mouth to bring him pleasure. Together they worked in tandem, sucking, licking, driving each other wild with hands and mouths.

"I will fill this ass one day, Joz." He licked her clit and trailed a finger over her ass.

Joz looked over her shoulder. "Reeva said you'd want to fuck my bootyhole." She rolled his balls in one hand while she pumped his dick with the other.

"Oh yes, I will fuck your bootyhole, and you'll love it. Not today, but soon." He pressed one finger into her ass, making her flinch then relax.

She laughed then turned back to his gorgeous cock. Pearly fluid leaked from the tip, the salty goodness something she could get addicted to. She felt his fingers slip into her vagina and then another into her ass. Oh, her mate was definitely gonna be claiming her bootyhole, and she was gonna be screaming his name when she came.

"Fuck, I'm gonna come, Turo," she gasped.

"That's a dirty mouth you got on you." He moved his fingers faster. "I like it. Come for me, Joz."

She wanted him to come with her. Her fingers slid between his thighs, saliva wetting them as she rubbed against his ass. He froze, but then, she swallowed as much of his cock as she could, feeling him bump the back of her throat and let her throat constrict around the head of him.

"Fuck, girl, what're you doing?" Turo's hips lifted, giving her access to slip her finger a little into him.

In the next heartbeat, he was coming down her throat. The fingers in her ass pistoned in and out, while his lips latched onto her clit and sucked, tossing her over the edge. She could do nothing but drink him down and come along with him.

Her body was still twitching when he lifted her off of him, tossing her onto her back and coming over her. She stared up at his dark eyes, eyes gone wild and hungry. "Fucking love you, Jozlyn. Stay with me forever."

His arms bracketed her head while he pushed his cock into her spasming pussy. God, how had she ever gone without this? Without Turo?

"We're complete together, Joz. Don't you feel it?" He stroked in and out, letting her feel the glide of his dick as he almost left her then the full force of his possession as he entered her again. "I don't just mean like this, but every way. You're in my heart, my mind, and my soul."

A tear streaked down the side of her face. "I feel the same. I'll never leave you now. And not because of your amazing fatty, although it is pretty great." She gasped as he pulled out and slammed back in.

"Woman, we are not calling Little T, fatty." He rolled his hips, hitting her clit with each brush of his pelvis.

She raised her brows. "Little T is better than fatty?"

Turo rolled them. "Shit, I don't care what you call him as long as you ride him."

Jozlyn lifted and then slammed back down, rolling her hips as she did. He felt even larger in this position. "Oh, Turo, I swear to god, you take my breath away. Fuck," she moaned as his hands gripped her hips and took over, lifting her up and down.

Words failed her. His cock rubbed against every nerve ending inside her. Long, fast, hard, every stroke he made spiked her arousal higher. A moan burst from her. The extreme pleasure was like nothing she'd ever experienced. She heard herself chanting his name. Felt him rubbing her clit as he rubbed the spot where she needed, ached the most, taking her higher.

"Yes, you feel fucking amazing, hahai. I'll never get enough of you, not even if I live for another three hundred years."

Joz, who had more words in her vocabulary than a single dictionary, couldn't think up an intelligent reply. Her mind fogged as it raced toward completion.

"You like it like this?" he asked rolling his hips.

Pleasure continued to build, words rolled from her, incoherent in their mumbled spillage as she begged him to do what she didn't know, only knew he was the only man who she wanted. She arched her hips and ground down on him. She felt a wildness, a crazy need to mark him, make him hers the same as he'd done to her.

A pulsating need thundered through her, maddening, like a frenzy escalating until she wasn't sure where she began, and he ended. The sensation pushed past any fear she had. She was empty, and only Turo could fill her.

"Yes, hahai, come for me," he ordered.

She bent down and took his earlobe between her teeth, nipping it then sliding down to his throat. "I love how you feel inside me," she panted.

Turo growled beneath her, the sound rumbled, shaking his body. "Take what you need. Take what is yours, mate."

This big strong man turned his neck and gave her his throat. Her wolf growled and struck in that moment. Sparks seemed to shower them, making her scream as satisfaction arced through her entire being, limb from limb coalescing into her center. The link between them became stronger. She saw the bands weave together as one, instead of two, braiding so tightly, his darker thread against her green and red.

Dimly she was aware Turo had found his own release, his shout of pleasure when she'd bitten him and the hot surge of his orgasm flooding her, triggered aftershocks inside her. Jolts still had tremors shaking her, reducing her to a limp mass of flesh.

"I bit you."

His gaze met hers, and he threw back his head and laughed. "Yes, my love you did, and it was exquisite."

Even now, totally spent her body still twitched. Of course, her mate held her on top of him, keeping them connected. "So, what now?"

Turo gripped one of her ass cheeks in his palm, the other he tugged her hair, making her look at him. "Now, we begin to live."

She placed a kiss over his chest, where his strong heart beat steady. "Yes, that sounds like a good plan. Wait 'til you meet my dad."

Her mate froze beneath her.

"Oh my, is the big bad wolf scared of meeting my daddy?" Joz joked.

Turo swallowed, his Adam's apple bobbed up and down. "I've never met my mate's family before."

"I get a first with you?" She felt undeniably excited by the news.

He tugged on her hair. "From this moment on, everything is a first with you. You'll be my first, my last, my everything. I've waited a lifetime for you, and I'd wait again, if it meant I'd have you, hahai. Please know you are exactly what I'd want in a mate."

She let the tears fall. "I'll try to be worthy of you. Be patient. It's hard when your mate is the most incredible man in the world, you know. I have a pretty high…" Turo stopped her words with a kiss that ended up with another toe-curling orgasm.

Two days later…

"Turo, my dad is not an ogre. Seriously, you're older than dirt and big as a house. Chill." Jozlyn straightened her skirt as Turo helped her out of his HellCat. Yes, he actually thought her dad would be more impressed if they didn't roar into their driveway in a big jacked-up truck. Instead, they roared up in a freaking limited-edition Dodge Challenger SRT HellCat.

Her parents stood on the porch, looking at them as they walked together hand-in-hand. She must say, Turo really did clean up well. Although, she did love him in holey jeans and a tank top, but seeing him in a pair of jeans, a button down, and a pair of Doc Martins really did do something to her. It made her want to mess them up is what it did.

"Stop that, woman," Turo whispered a few feet from their parents.

"Stop what?" she asked.

He inhaled, giving her all the answer she needed. Goodness, her man was hell on her good girl senses.

"Jozlyn, it's so good to see you. This must be the young man you told us about." Her mother Noriko held her arms open.

Joz let go of Turo and went up the steps to greet her parents.

Turo watched his mate greet her parents. He also took in the stance of Patrick Rasey and his watchful stare. Joz had said her dad was retired but still travelled with work. She wasn't sure what he did now, only knew he was gone a lot. Turo would bet his left nut the man was ex-military and still had his hand in it somehow.

He went up to the porch and held his hand out to her father. "Mr. Rasey. It's a pleasure to meet you."

Joz's father looked him up and down then took his hand. The firm grip let Turo know more than words that he wasn't a pencil pusher, nor was he gonna let just any man take his baby girl. Oh, not that there was a snowball's chance in hell he'd give Joz up, but he would put her parents at ease.

"Arturo Anoa'i. Where you from, boy?" Patrick's green eyes pinned Turo.

"Daddy," Joz pleaded.

"Why don't we go inside before the formal, whatever you plan to do is done, Pat," Noriko said.

Turo laughed. "It's okay, hahai, I'd do the same if you were my only daughter."

Patrick grunted. "Come on in. Noriko, why don't you and Joz get us a drink and let me have a moment with our daughter's young man in my study."

He'd imagined how many times fathers had done something similar and couldn't wait to see Patrick in action. He held his hand up as Joz opened her mouth. "I'll be fine." Bending quickly, he kissed her cheek, not wanting to tick her father off.

Jozlyn's father led him into his office and shut the door. Turo looked around at the masculine room, studying the layout and letting his wolf senses check for danger. He smelled gun powder and lead. Yeah, as he suspected, Patrick wasn't a paper pusher.

"What are your intentions with my girl?" Patrick got down to the only question he clearly wanted answered.

Turo put his hands in his pockets. "I plan to be with her for the rest of my life, sir." He watched as Patrick's eyes registered the title.

"What gave me away?"

"You carry yourself like a military man. I run a military training course of a sort where men and women come to learn to shoot guns and for target practice. I've been around military men and women for a...long time." He was going to say a lot longer than Patrick had been alive but stopped himself in time.

They talked about guns. What their favorite one was and made plans for Patrick to come to his training course. "Now, just so we're clear. You hurt my baby girl, and I'll kill you. I'm an excellent marksman," Patrick warned.

Turo didn't let the father of his mate know that he was better. Hell, the world record was just beat with a sniper shooting his target at 3,871 yds, but Turo could hit a target even further with precision. Nope, he'd keep that info to himself.

"Well, I guess since there's no yelling then all is good in here," Jozlyn said as she walked in with a glass of juice in each hand.

He took one from her, quirking a brow. "Daddy can be scary."

Her father snorted. "Your mother's the scary one."

Noriko stuck her head in. "Lunch is ready if you're done trying to be macho."

Turo met the dark eyes of Joz's mom and nearly dropped the drink. For a moment, he could swear she saw through to his wolf, but then she blinked and turned away. Being a member of the Rasey's was definitely going to be a new experience for Turo. He just hoped her parents were ready for him. They spent the next couple hours getting to know him, while he subtly read them. Of course, he felt the gentle touch of her mother trying to get inside his mind, but he didn't allow her to see more than his love for her daughter. By the time they were standing to leave, he was sure her parents weren't nearly as suspicious of him and his intentions toward their only child.

Turo started his car, the deep rumble reminded him of an angry animal. He loved it, "I like your parents."

Joz nodded. "They liked you too. My father is all bark and no bite."

He snorted. "Sweetheart, I think your dad is a little more than you think. I'm gonna take him to my training course and let him have a little fun. I think it would be good for you to see your dad in action."

"What? I don't think my dad even knows how to shoot a gun." Joz patted his hand.

The following week Turo took Joz and her father, along with Noriko, to his training course. He'd made sure nobody else had reserved it, wanting to have the entire course for his mate and her family.

Patrick walked out wearing Khaki pants and shirt. The kind you'd see on a nature show. Turo rolled his eyes at the man and waited until he'd helped Joz's mother into his big truck. "Are you over compensating for something, Arturo?" Patrick asked as he sat in the back.

Turo laughed. "No, sir, and I'll leave it at that, since you're gonna have a gun later."

"Smart boy."

When they got to the course, Joz and her mother stared in awe as Patrick assembled an assault rifle from one of the cases he'd loaded into the truck. The course was made up of different settings, each one unique in whatever the participant's needs were. By the time they finished the third course, Joz and Noriko had their arms crossed, glaring at Patrick.

"These trips, what do you do?" Noriko asked.

Patrick put his gun away. "I consult with the military. I teach young men how to shoot through video games, but I also go out and shoot in obstacle courses too. However, none are on par with this. This, Turo, is spectacular."

"Don't try to butter him up, Patrick Rasey." Noriko tapped her toe on the concrete floor. "Have you been in danger at all in the times you've left?"

He held his hands up. "Sweetheart, I promise I was never in any danger."

Turo inhaled, scenting no lie.

"Fine, but we have some major talking to do, mister. Turo, can you take us home?"

Joz smiled. She knew that tone and could tell her father was totally gonna be kissing up for the next day or so. "You're in trouble." She wagged her finger at her father.

"Don't sass me, young lady. I think that man of yours is going to be just what the doctor ordered for my little girl. Just don't mess it up, Arturo, or you won't be a happy soldier."

Turo grinned. He'd thought of all the romantic things he could do for his mate. In their world, they were mated for life, a bond that was stronger than any marriage vows. However, she still had ties to the human world with her parents. He put his hand in his pocket then got down on one knee in front of Joz. "Jozlyn, I know I won't always do or say the right thing. Things won't always be perfect. I'll fuck up, cuss at the wrong time. But through all the bad, I'll love you harder than anybody else. I don't deserve you. You're too damn good for an old wolf like me, but I'll make sure every day you have a reason to smile, just like you've given me a reason. Will you do me the honor of making an honest man of me?"

Joz sniffed as tears streaked down her face. "Gosh darn you, Turo, I swore I wouldn't cry if you asked me to marry you."

His brow furrowed. "Ko'u uuku hahai, if those are happy tears I'll work to make those the only ones you ever cry again."

"He just called her his little butterfly. Isn't that romantic?" Noriko asked to her husband.

Patrick grunted. "Yeah, but he better keep his promise. Wolf indeed."

Joz took the ring from Turo, the platinum band had a solid diamond ringed with smaller diamonds all around it. "Yes, yes I'll marry you."

"Thank fuck," Turo growled, standing and swinging Joz into his arms.

"I think that's one of those inappropriate cussing times," Patrick mumbled.

Noriko slapped her hand over his mouth. "We'll give you two a moment alone."

Turo wiped the wetness off her cheeks. "You like the ring?"

"I love it, but I didn't need it to belong to you." She wrapped her legs around Turo. "I want to fuck you so bad right now."

"Goddess, you with your potty mouth. Do you know how much that turns me on, and your parents are right over there?" he groaned burying his face against her neck, licking the mating mark only other shifters could see and sense. She shuddered in his arms. He'd have to learn to watch what he said around the elder Rasey's as he'd slipped up and called himself a wolf. Thankfully, they didn't question his wording.

"Let's take my parents' home then I'll show you how much I love my ring."

He looked down at his mate and kissed her quickly. "I want to make love to you with you wearing only my ring."

She smiled, love shining brightly from her dark eyes. "Sounds like the best plan ever."

The End

Want to read how it all began? Check out Lyric's Accidental Mate

Iron Wolves MC book 1
CHECK IT OUT HERE

The Iron Wolves Next Generation is Here!

Check out Bad Wolf, Book 1

If you enjoyed this book, you may also enjoy…

The Mystic Wolves Series

The Magic and Mayhem Series

The Ravens of War Series

The Complete Iron Wolves Series Here

Signup For My Newsletter For Accidentally Wolf, Book 1 of the Mystic Wolves

About Elle Boon

Elle Boon is a reader first and foremost...and of course if you know her, she's the crazy lady with purple hair. She's also a USA Today Bestselling Author who lives in Middle-Merica as she likes to say...with her husband and Kally Kay, her black lab who also thinks she's her writing partner. (She happens to sit next to her begging for treats and so takes a lot of credit). She has two amazing kids, Jazz and Goob, and is a MiMi to one adorable little nugget named Romy or RomyGirl (greatest job EVER) who has totally won over everyone who sees hers (If anyone says a hair bow is too big, they're crazy). She's known for saying "Bless Your Heart" and dropping lots of F-bombs (I mean lots of F-BOMBS, but who is keeping track?).

She loves where this new journey has taken her and has no plans on stopping. She writes what she loves to read, and that's romance, whether it's about Navy SEALs, HOT as F**K MC heroes, or paranormal alphas. #dontlookdown is a thing you will need to google. "Wink" With all her stories, you're guaranteed a happily ever after, no matter what twisted thing her mind has come up with. Her biggest hope is that after readers have read one of her stories, they fall in love with her characters as much as she has. She loves creating new worlds and has more just waiting to be written. Elle believes in happily ever after and can guarantee you will always get one within the pages of her books.

Connect with Elle online. She loves to hear from you:

www.elleboon.com

https://www.facebook.com/elle.boon

https://www.facebook.com/Elle-Boon-Author-1429718517289545/

https://twitter.com/ElleBoon1

https://www.facebook.com/groups/RacyReads/

https://www.facebook.com/groups/1405756769719931/

https://www.goodreads.com/author/show/8120085.Elle_Boon

https://www.bookbub.com/authors/elle-boon

https://www.instagram.com/elleboon/

http://www.elleboon.com/newsletter

Other Books by Elle Boon

Ravens of War
Selena's Men
Two For Tamara
Jaklyn's Saviors
Kira's Warriors
Akra's Demons
Nita's Redemption

Mystic Wolves
Accidentally Wolf
His Perfect Wolf
Jett's Wild Wolf
Bronx's Wounded Wolf
A Fey's Wolf
Their Wicked Wolf
Atlas's Forbidden Wolf

SmokeJumpers
FireStarter
Berserker's Rage
A SmokeJumpers Christmas
Choosing His Mate, A Prequel to FireStarter

Iron Wolves MC
Lyric's Accidental Mate
Xan's Feisty Mate
Kellen's Tempting Mate

Slater's Enchanted Mate
Creed's Dark Lovers
Bodhi's Synful Mate
Turo's Fated Mate
Jenna's Dark Mates
Arynn's Chosen Mate
Coti's Unclaimed Mate

Miami Nights
Miami Inferno
Rescuing Miami

Standalone
Wild and Dirty, Wild Irish Series
Big Deal Sweetheart

SEAL Team Phantom Series
Delta Salvation
Delta Recon
Delta Rogue
Delta Redemption
Mission Saving Shayna
Protecting Teagan

The Royal Sons MC Series
Royally Twisted
Royally Taken

Royally Tempted
Royally Treasured
Royally Broken
Royally Saved
Royally Chosen Christmas
Royally Beloved
Royally Targeted
Royally Inked
Royally Destroyed, Coming 2023

Magic and Mayhem
The Lion's Witchy Mate
The Leopards Witchy Mate

Standalone
Shaw's Wild Mate, Coming Soon

A Cursed Hallows Eve Anthology
Their Dragon Mate
Her Dragon Mate
The Dragon's Mate

IRON WOLVES THE NEXT GENERATION
Bad Wolf – *Xian Book 1*
Tempted Wolf – *Jagger Book 2*

The Vampire's Wolf – Liv & Kahn
Book 3
Embrace A Wolf – Jaxon Book 4